ROMANCE DUST

FROM

THE HISTORIC PLACER.

BY

WILLIAM STARBUCK MAYO, M. D.

AUTHOR OF "KALOOLAH," "THE BERBER," "ILLUSTRATIONS OF NATURAL PHILOSOPHY," &c. &c. &c.

NEW-YORK:
GEO. P. PUTNAM, 155 BROADWAY.

LONDON:
RICHARD BENTLEY, NEW BURLINGTON-STREET.

1851.

Stereotyped and Printed
BY D. FANSHAW,
35 Ann, corner of Nassau-st.

CONTENTS.

PREFACE.

"Romance Dust from the Historic Placer! A far-fetched title!"

True, it was brought, after many excursions of fancy round the world, and round the world in search of a name that would exactly hit every reader's taste, from no less distant a land than the new El Dorado. If you knew how difficult it is sometimes to find an expressive and original title for a book of this kind—a book which does not necessarily suggest a title from itself—you would not object to the distance. Picking up perfectly fitting and taking titles, is about as easy as picking up gold purses and diamond rings from the pavements of New-York or London: such things do exist, but fifty chances to one, you will find some sharp-eyed or quick-fancied fellow is before-hand with you, and has them snugly stowed away in his pockets or pages.

But, perhaps, it is not the distance from which my unlucky specimen comes, that you object to! No; it is not so much that, but "you don't like to see an author rush across the Isthmus of propriety, in his agony to avoid the Atlantic of common place, and plunging into the Pacific of novelty, bring up some miserable metaphorical nondescript, instead of a pearl of purity and price." Certainly not, but it must be recollected—still sticking to a California figure—that the best divers in the Gulf cannot always be sure of their oysters, and that when they find no pearls, they content themselves with the *nacre*—they bring home the shells—and the shells "pay." Now, this specimen may not be of the clearest water, but I am induced to think, that upon opening the following pages, you will open the metaphor, and find, if not a true pearl, at least mother o' pearl enough for a very decent handle to the book.

So much for the name, about which I should have said nothing, had I not received an intimation from a most distinguished literary authority, that my title smacked of affectation, and was therefore not in the best taste. Unluckily, it was already printed in the running head to the pages, and could not be changed.

Two or three of the shorter articles were prepared long ago; the others have been recently written, partly to use up a portion of the historical materials left over from Kaloolah and The Berber; partly as a diversion to more serious labor, and partly to keep afloat in the ocean of print until such time as a bark of more pretension is ready to be launched.

DON SEBASTIAN.

A TALE FROM THE CHRONICLES OF PORTUGAL.

CHAPTER I.

"Gallant and gay in Lisbon's bay, with streamers flaunting wide,
"Upon the gleaming waters, Sebastian's galleys ride,
"His valorous armada, (was never nobler sight!)
"Hath young Sebastian marshalled against the Moorish might."

In the year 1125 the Moorish dominion in Portugal received its death-blow from the hands of Alphonso I. in the bloody field of Ourique. The Moors, however, continued the desperate struggle for many years, until, in the time of Alphonso III. they were expelled from their last strongholds in the province of Algarve, and the kingdom, following the example of its neighbor Spain, was purged from the presence of the infidel, and restored to Christian rule. The expulsion of the Moors, however, by no means lessened the enmities, or closed the contests between the followers of the crescent and the cross; and the chronicles of two centuries of unceasing warfare by land and sea, attest on every page the intensity of their mutual hate. The

Moors, driven from Portugal, found a home with their brethren of Morocco. Sympathy with their sufferings added fuel to the fire which, from the time of Gebel Tarak had been blazing in their breasts, and a degree of religious and national animosity was aroused, more intense than was ever felt by the earlier Saracens, and which has descended in all its bitterness, even to the present day

Such were the relations of the two countries when, in the year 1556, died John III. leaving his grandson, Don Sebastian, a child three years old, heir to the throne. By the King's will, the Queen mother was appointed regent She, however, after having by her energy compelled the Moors to raise the siege of Mazagan, a Portuguese possession upon the coast of Morocco, which had been invested by the King of Fas, with eighty thousand men, resigned the regency into the hands of the cardinal infant, Don Henry. Under the cardinal the Jesuits acquired unbounded influence. Don Alexius de Meneses was appointed the young King's governor, and Gonzales de Camera, with two other priests, his preceptors. By them he was early taught that a reverence for the church, military courage, and hatred of Mahometans, were the principal duties of his station. As he grew up he was disabused of some of his prejudices in favor of the Jesuits, by Alcacora, his principal secretary of state, and by the noble Don Alvaro de Castro; but his detestation of the Moors increased with his growth, until it bore its bitter fruits in the fatal battle of Alccassarquivir, where perished the choicest chivalry of Portugal and Spain, and where was struck a deadly blow at Portuguese freedom and power.

Don Sebastian having attained his majority, and assumed the reigns of government, resolved to gratify his strongest passion, and, at the same time, fulfil what he conceived a sacred duty, by conducting an expedition against the Moors. It happened at this time that Muley Hamet, the legitimate King of Morocco, had been dispossessed of his throne by his uncle Muley Molock. He applied to Don Sebastian for assistance, and as an inducement to grant him the aid he sought, he caused Azila, a town of which he was master, to be given up to the Portuguese. Don Sebastian needed no encouragement to take advantage of the opportunity, and he at once announced his determination to commence a war with the Moors. Philip II. of Spain, whose daughter had been promised to Don Sebastian, exerted himself to oppose the young King's resolution: he represented the difficulties and the dangers of an invasion of Morocco—the almost certainty of ultimate defeat, and the inutility even of victory. Finding, however, that it was impossible to change Sebastian's determination, he engaged to assist him with fifty galleys and five thousand men, and Francesco Aldana, an old and experienced officer, was despatched to Morocco by Philip, to gather information for Sebastian.

Many of the most influential men of the Portuguese

court were strongly opposed to the expedition. The Queen-dowager used the most urgent entreaties, and the cardinal, Don Henry, strenuously endeavored to dissuade the young King from his purpose, but he was alike deaf to the warnings of his uncle and the solicitations of his mother. The Emperor, Muley Molock, addressed him a letter, deprecating his martial fury and religious zeal, but to no effect. The preparations for the invasion were urg. ed forward with renewed ardor. All Portugal resounded with the note of preparation for the expedition, and all Europe was filled with its fame.

The seventeenth of June, 1577, was a day of unusual commotion and excitement in the city of Lisbon. It had been appointed for the consecration of the royal banner, which, for the purpose, was to be carried in grand procession to the cathedral church of *Noso Senhora.* At an early hour, small bodies of troops in gallant array, with music sounding, standards waving, and their polished armor flashing in the brilliant sunlight, commenced debouching into the beautiful square, now the *Praca do Commercio*, then the esplanade of the royal palace.

In the balconies of the lower end of the vast audience hall, which overlooked the square, stood a group of gay and gallant cavaliers, conspicuous among whom were the graceful and chivalric Duke of Aveyro, and Don Diego, and Don John, the youthful sons of the Duke of Braganza. The appearance of the troops, the antics of the populace, and the crowds of mantillas crowding the balconies and house-tops commanding a view of the square, occupied the attention, and afforded much amusement to the lounging nobles, who were awaiting the appearance of the King.

"*Por Dios!* I wish the Moor could catch a glimpse of this scene," exclaimed young Don John, "and yet I should be sorry if he could; the infidel would be frightened into the *Saharah*, and victory would be bloodless and inglorious."

"It is well that your father heard not that remark," replied Don Antonio, Prior of Crato—a grave and dignified noble. "Braganza's sword has a thousand times been dyed in the blood of the Moor, but it never found him a coward. We can add nothing to our own valor by disparaging that of our enemies."

"I meant not to say that the infidel is a coward," returned Don John, "but if he is as brave as Sancho, his courage will avail him naught. I feel that if we can once set foot in El Garb, we shall smite him to more purpose than Signor Samson, whom Father Gonzales was telling us about the other day, did the Philistines."

"Ha! look! there come the Germans with that grim looking, old Colonel Amberg at their head," interposed Don Diego.

"Yes," exclaimed Don John, "and here come the

Italians with their English commander, Sir Thomas Stukely. He's a gallant fellow, but I wish he and all the other foreigners had staid at home. We want them not, and they will only share our glory."

"Nay, nay! be not so greedy of glory, my young friend," replied the Duke of Areyro. "There is no danger that the swords of our allies will not leave Moors enough for your weapon."

"How many do the foreigners number? inquired the Prior of Crato of the Duke.

"The Prince of Orange furnishes a corps of three thousand Germans; and an efficient body they are. The King of Spain sends Alonzo Aquilar with two thousand Castilians, the very flower of chivalry. Five hundred volunteers have ranged themselves under the banner of Don Christopher Tavora. We might have given them an abler leader, although not a braver. These are all except the seven hundred Italians Stukely has contrived to collect. They are regular dare-devils, who would follow their leader to the infernal regions, and he is just the one to go if he only knew the way, and thought he could find any booty. But who can this be?" exclaimed the Duke, directing the attention of his companions to a cavalier, who, with a small retinue was approaching the palace.

"He looks like the Spaniard Aldana. It must be him; now we shall hear some news from Morocco."

The stranger dismounted at the gate of the palace,

passed the guard with the usual formalities, and was ushered into the hall.

"Welcome! Francesco Aldana!" burst from a dozen voices as he entered, and the impatient and curious nobles thronged around him to congratulate him upon his return from Africa, whither it was known that he had been despatched by the king of Spain. Before, however, he could reply to their numerous questions, the approach of the King was announced.

The doors at the upper end of the hall was thrown open, and Don Sebastian, attended by the cardinal Don Henry, entered the room. His appearance was majestic in the extreme. Far above the common size, he was well proportioned and graceful; his features were finely formed, his eyes blue, and the expression of his face pleasing and dignified. Possessing prodigious personal strength, he excelled in all military and gymnastic exercises, and despite the faults of his education, he had many virtues which eminently fitted him for the throne. The chroniclers of his time describe him as "incapable of fear, magnificent, generous, affable, full of justice, piety, and truth."

Advancing into the centre of the hall, the King and the cardinal seemed wholly absorbed in the subject of their conversation, which, from the deep frown upon the King's brow, it was evident was far from being pleasing to him. Breaking away at length with a gesture of angry impatience, he exclaimed in a tone that startled the assembled nobles—

"No! *Por Dios*, no! I tell thee, most noble uncle and holy father; another week will see my departure from the Tagus. Ha! Francesco Aldana, my old and gallant soldier, right welcome. Whence come you now? You are from Morocco, I suppose."

"I have this moment arrived from Madrid," replied Aldana, "to which city I returned three days since, from the mission to Africa, of which your majesty has been apprized."

"Well, what news of the Paynim hounds? What think they of our purpose? I warrant they hold it not so lightly as some of our ease-loving subjects."

"The news I bring, I am sorry to inform your majesty, is not so favorable as I could wish, but it was deemed of so much importance by my royal master, that he ordered me to bring it myself with all despatch. The real object of my visit was suspected, and I was debarred from many opportunities of personal observation, but by correspondence with the Spanish priests, who are allowed to reside in Africa, I obtained all necessary information. The most active preparations have been made to resist your invasion. Muley Molock has raised a force of sixty thousand horse, and forty thousand foot, and the garrisons of all the towns have been strengthened. The King, my master, has directed me to inform your majesty of these facts, and to explain that the nature of the country is a still more formidable obstacle to military operations. He orders me to beg that your majesty will listen to the opinion of one who, however unworthy of the honor, has been styled by his most gracious master, his most experienced soldier."

"Now, *Por todos los Santos*," interrupted the King, "it would seem there has been formed a right pretty league to interrupt my purpose. First, there is my good mother with her womanly alarms, daily endeavoring to dissuade me, then here is my most noble uncle, the cardinal, and thirdly, my royal cousin, and promised father-in-law of Spain. Truly, a right noble league; but with me it avails not; I falter not in my determination. The difficulties and dangers, were they ten times greater, appal not me. Why should the Portuguese of to-day be afraid to emulate the exploits of their ancestors, who have written so often in the blood of the Moor, their titles to immortality? Are we not," continued the King, his voice rising, and his countenance kindling with excitement, "are we not," he exclaimed, glancing his flashing eye along the line of nobles, "the descendants of Alphonzo, and Sancho, and Alonzo, and Briganza, Coutigno, and Narvarra, and their glorious compeers, who rescued this fair land from the infidel dogs, and who planted the banners of Portugal upon the battlements of Tangier and Mazagan, where they still triumphantly float, mocking the efforts of the Moor?

What say you; shall we yield to the solicitations of our cautious friends, or shall we fling abroad our standard to the breeze, and sword in hand, strike one good blow for honor and the cross? Speak!" he exclaimed, drawing his sword, "speak, who joins me in the cry of *vengeance on the Moor!*"

In an instant a hundred swords leaped from their scabbards and flashed in the glittering sunlight, and a shout that seemed to rend the palace, reverberated through the arches of the lofty hall. "Vengeance on the Moor! Vengeance on the Moor!" It ceased, but it had already passed the portals, and was taken up by the multitudes who crowded the *placa*, and from a hundred thousand throats was repeated, "*Morao os Mouros! Viva o Rey! Morao os Mouros!*"

"To horse! to horse! gentlemen," exclaimed the King. "We must not keep our holy father of Guarda waiting."

Attended by all the officers of state, the King placed himself at the head of the procession, which took up its line of march for the church of *Noso Senhora*, situated opposite the vast and gloomy pile of the Inquisition, forming one side of the *Praca Roca.*

CHAPTER II.

> There are a thousand barons, all harnessed cap-a-pee,
> "With helm and spear that glitter clear, above the dark green sea;
> "No lack of gold and silver to stamp each proud device
> "On shield or surcoat—nor of chains and jewelry of price."

We need not describe the imposing ceremonial of the consecration. The royal standard having been blessed by the archbishop, was presented to the King, who instantly handed it to Don Lewis de Menesis, with orders for the immediate embarkation of the troops. One week was consumed in this operation, and on the twenty-fourth of June, the whole fleet, consisting of fifty ships of war, and five gallies, accompanied by transports and tenders, amounting to a thousand sail, weighed anchor from the Tagus. Stopping at Cadiz, the King was royally entertained by the magnificent Duke Medina Sidonia, who, by direction of the King of Spain, made a last effort, but without effect, to dissuade Don Sebastian from his purpose. After waiting a week at Cadiz for some reinforcements, the fleet again got under way, the main body with the troops, and a train of twelve pieces of cannon, proceeding, by order of the King, under Don Diego de Sousa, to Azila, a town upon the Atlantic coast, about twenty miles from the mouth of the Straits of

Gibraltar, while the King himself, with a detachment of troops, directed his course to Tangier. Here he was joined by the sherife, Muley Hamet, the deposed Emperor of Morocco, with a body of three hundred horse. The sherife delivered up his son, Muley, a boy of twelve years of age, to the King, who sent him as a hostage to Mazagan. After a stay of three weeks in Tangier, the King, accompanied by Hamet, joined his army at Azila, where it was concluded in a council of war to reduce El Arache, but whether to march thither by land, or to embark the troops and proceed by sea, led to a long debate, which was finally decided by the King in favor of the march by land, and orders were given to advance directly to the River Lucos. This measure was opposed by Muley Hamet, but the King gave him so rude an answer, that he left Sebastian's presence in discontent. On the twenty-ninth the army commenced its march, and encamped two leagues from Azila, where it was joined by Aldana, who presented him with a letter from the Duke of Alva, begging him to undertake nothing beyond the capture of El Arache, and the recovery of a helmet formerly worn by Charles V.

In the meantime the Emperor Molock had not been idle. With an army of an hundred thousand men he marched from Morocco, and on the third of August he encamped about a league from Alcassarquivir, and within sight of the Christian troops. Suspicious of the fidelity of some of his troops, and particularly of his officers, whom he thought likely to be bribed by Portuguese gold, he changed the disposition of his army, so that none of his officers commanded the corps which had been under their orders, and having new men to deal with, had, consequently, none whom they could trust. As soon as the scouts of the Moorish army were perceived, a council of war was convened in the Christian camp, in which it was decided to give battle on the morrow, contrary to the advice of Hamet, who, learning that Muley Molock was dangerously ill, was confident that in the event of his death, the greater part of the Moorish soldiery would come over to their legitimate commander.

The morning of the fourth dawned upon a scene of unusual splendor. Rising from the plain of Alcassar were the whitewashed walls and battlements of the town; to the east extended the blue ridge of Atlas; to the west Jebbel Subah, or Lion's Mount, supported the snowy tombs of several renowned saints; and separated by the almost dry bed of the river Lucos, were the opposing armies.

On one side a sea of turbaned heads, on the other, helmets and waving plumes and fluttering pinions. Con spicuous above all, was Sebastian, who, with Aldana by his side, galloped throughout the field, he himself marshalling the lines, and attending to the minutest disposition of his men, and clear above the clash of arms, the tramp of cavalry, and the hoarse orders of his officers, arose the trumpet tones of the youthful King. The Christians were far inferior in number to the Moors, but never was Paynim host confronted by a more gallant force—never was there collected a greater proportion of veteran officers and noble knights.

At 11 o'clock, P. M. a general discharge of the Moorish artillery gave the signal for battle. In an instant an answering roar burst from the mouths of the Christian cannon.

"Charge!" shouted the impatient Don, "upon them under cover of the smoke! Follow me!"

At the head of the volunteers, the King dashed forward against the centre of the first Moorish line. The Andalusians recoiled before the impetuous valor of the youthful Don. Borne back by the resistless shock of the fierce nobles of which the band of volunteers was wholly composed, they were, for a few moments, completely broken and scattered, but at length, by the advance of the renegados, they rallied, and by their superiority in numbers, were enabled to stand their ground.

The fight became a confused and desperate *melée.*

"God and the king! death to the infidel!" shouted the Christians. "Allah il Allah! down with the *kaffirs!*" answered the Moors. Swords and cimetars rose and fell, adding their ringing clash to the tumult of the strife.

Aldana, Gonzalez, Chacon, and Alonzo Aquila, all Castilians, were stricken down by the King's side. In a moment he himself was brought to the ground by the fall of his horse. George Albuquerque gallopped up, sprang from his steed, and offered it to his royal master.

"How goes it?" demanded the King.

"All is lost. Both the Moorish wings have taken us in flank, and the Portuguese have given way. I beseech your Majesty to fly while there is yet time."

"Fly! never. Let us die upon this," exclaimed Don Sebastian, seizing his standard, and wrapping its folds around his person, he spurred into the thickest of the fight. Felling an infidel at every blow, he was at last borne to the ground by the sheer force of numbers. At this moment, at the head of a few nobles, Louis de Britto made a charge upon the spot where last the plume of the King was seen to wave. He caught a glimpse of the fallen monarch, but was unable to effect his rescue.

This, it was asserted by many, was the last time he was ever seen alive, but as all attempts to verify his death proved abortive, a very general opinion obtained that he had escaped with his life, and events sometime after occurred to justify the popular belief.

CHAPTER III.

"I stood in Venice on the bridge of Sighs
"A palace and a prison on each hand."

A few words will suffice for a period of twenty years, which we must now suppose to have elapsed since the date of the events related in the preceding chapters.

A woful day in Portugal was that in which the tidings of the battle of Alcassarquivir were received. There was not a noble family in the kingdom which had not its representative in the fatal fight. The flower of her chivalry destroyed, and the resources of the kingdom exhausted, her political independence received its death-blow, and she soon fell an easy prey to the insatiable ambition of her rival, Spain.

The Cardinal Don Henry succeeded to the throne. At his death, after a short reign of two years, Philip II. of Spain, laid a claim to the crown, which he succeeded in enforcing, and Portugal was annexed to his dominions.

A mission was despatched by Philip to Morocco, to negotiate for the ransom of the prisoners. Captain Zuniga was the minister appointed, who succeeded in making a treaty of alliance, and in liberating without ransom, the Duke of Barcelos, and the Spanish ambassador. The supposed body of Don Sebastian was likewise given up. It was taken from Alcassarquivir, where it had been deposited, to Ceuta, and from thence to Lisbon, where it was buried with great pomp in the royal vaults, in the monastery of Belem.

Even this, however, failed to satisfy the Portuguese of the death of their beloved king. Rumors were rife that he had been seen alive, and the people lived in daily expectation of his coming to deliver them from the hated Castilian yoke.

Induced by this conviction of the public mind, the son of a tailor, of Alcobaza, undertook to personate the expected Don. He had two companions, one who represented himself to be Don Christopher di Tavora, the other, the Bishop of Guarda. They were apprehended and led through the streets of Lisbon. The false Sebastian was sent to the gallies, and the bishop was hanged.

Not long after this, a new pretender appeared in the person of Gonzalo Alvares, the son of a mason. Having promised marriage to the daughter of Pedro Alonzo, a rich farmer, whom he created earl of Torres Novas, he assembled a body of eight hundred men—considerable blood was spilt before he was apprehended. It was clearly established that he was an impostor, and with his intended father-in-law he was hanged and quartered at Lisbon.

Our story, as we have said, now takes the reader at one step, not only over a period of twenty years, but transfers him in imagination to a new and distant scene—a scene

"Where Venice sat in state throned on her hundred isles."

It was a bright Italian day, and every living thing in the then chief commercial mart of the world, seemed to feel its invigorating influence. From all sides arose the busy hum of industry—the shout—the laugh—the song. A thousand barges were lading at the warehouse doors, their precious cargoes of Indian goods. Myriads of gondolas were skimming with graceful rapidity the surface of the numerous canals, and crowds of citizens and foreigners of every language, color and costume, jostled each other on the *Rìalto*, and in the *Piazza de San Marco*. But something in the looks—the gestures and the speech of the assembled multitude in St. Mark's betokened some unusual cause of excitement—a knowledge of which may perhaps be best conveyed in the following dialogue, which took place between a Portuguese resident of Venice, and his friend from Lisbon, who had just arrived:

"But hast thou heard the news?" exclaimed Pedro Varro to Alonzo Carrara, after the first friendly greetings had been exchanged, as they stood beneath the arcade of the *Procuratie Nuona*, a pile of buildings which had just been erected.

"News! no, what news? I heard the name of Don Sebastian lauded by fifty voices as I made my way from the *Sestiere de Cunareggio.* It can't be that there is any thing new of the defunct Don."

"There is, and not more marvellous than true. Thy journeyings must have been far, indeed, not to have heard of what has given them more trouble at Madrid than the haughty Castilian would like to own. That this is no Gonzalo Alvares affair, my own eyes can testify. Come, step aside from this crowd, and I will tell thee the story."

"Thou knowest," he resumed, "with what confidence the people of Portugal have expected the re-appearance of Don Sebastian. Well, at last he has arrived. I have seen him, I know that it is he. He came to Venice several weeks since. The account that he gives of himself is, that he saved his life by hiding himself among the slain until night had veiled the field of Alcassarquivir. After wandering for three days with no definite object, without food and in momentary danger of detection, he had the good fortune to aid a Berber chieftain, who was flying from the Moors, and to secure his protection. He affirms that a year after the battle, he made his way secretly by the aid of his Berber friend from Africa to Algarve, that he gave notice of his return to the king, Don Henry, and that the only answers he received, were repeated attempts to assassinate him, in consequence of which, and being unwilling to disturb the peace of the country, he returned to his friends in Africa. You doubtless recollect a rumor in Lisbon at the time, that Don Sebastian had been seen in Algarve?"

"I recollect it well," replied Carrara, "and it may well be that the King Don Henry knew it to be true. He was not one to willingly yield up the crown and resume his cardinal's hat."

"True! if, however, he had known how short a time he had to wear them, he would not have cared much for either," replied Varro, who resumed his story.

"After living for several years in Africa, passing from place to place in the habit of a penitent, the king came to Sicily, where, for a long time, he led the life of a hermit, but at length he felt it his duty to go to Rome and tell his story to the Holy Father. On his way, he was robbed, which, for the time, diverted him from his purpose, and he arrived in this city. He was at once recognized by several of our friends. The story spread. Complaint was made by the Spanish ambassador to the senate, and he was ordered to leave the city. He went to Padua, but the governor, fearful of Spanish anger, drove him forth, when he was compelled to return to this city, and was imprisoned. He underwent twenty-eight examinations before a committee of nobles, in which were elicited the facts which I have stated, and in which he proved himself guiltless of the crimes which the Spaniard endeavored to fasten upon him."

"And the committee, what decision did it pronounce?"

"None, but they showed no disposition to declare him an impostor. The senate decided that they would not discuss the great point whether he was the real Don unless they were requested to do so by some prince or state in alliance with them. They were compelled to do so by the prince of Orange, who sent Don Christopher to make the request. Yesterday the solemn examination was concluded, but with no result. They dared not say yes, and they could not say no, so they have ordered that Sebastian be set at liberty, and that he leave the city in three days."

"The cowards!" exclaimed Carrara, "that is throwing him directly into the jaws of the Spaniard."

"Hush!" replied Varro, "beware the lion of St. Marks. To-night we meet to devise measures for his escape. It is proposed to send him to Padua, disguised as a monk. Meet me an hour to sunset in the *Mereciria*, and I will tell thee further of our plans."

* * * * * * * *

Again, for the sake of preserving a proper brevity in our marvellous but true tale, must we beg the reader to step with us over an interval of time and space.

It was in the heart of Castile, upon a projecting, almost inaccessible point of the *Sierra D'Occa*, that was situated the strong castle Pirynera, once the habitation of a race of Gothic chieftains, it had become the property of the crown, and was never used, except occasionally, as a prison for offenders against the state.

In one of the deepest dungeons of this gloomy fortress, upon a pallet of straw, reclined a dying prisoner. Though not yet fifty years of age, sorrow and toil had anticipated time's gentle footsteps. The marks of age were strongly stamped upon the deeply wrinkled brow, the care-worn, haggard face, and in the snow-white hair and beard. Death, his kindest friend, was close at hand, yet still from that sunk eye and pallid cheek, gleamed an expression of calm, majestic piety and patience, which in all his toils and trouble had ever been his chief characteristic. He gasped for breath, which was painfully supplied by the damp air of his dungeon. The cold drops stood upon his brow, he felt the icy fingers of the friend he had often invoked, around his throbbing heart.

"Can I do aught for thee?" inquired a rough but kindly spoken man, who stood beside the prisoner.

"Nothing, Pereco, but the priest, I would fain see the priest once more."

"I will seek him," replied the man he addressed, who was evidently a novice in the indurating profession of jailor.

Leaving the gloomy cell, which was dimly illuminated by the feeble rays of a single lamp, he ascended by a narrow winding stone staircase to the region of light and day.

"How is the prisoner?" demanded a hard featured grim looking man—the governor of the castle and commander of the dozen soldiers, to whose care it was entrusted.

"How is the prisoner—I hope he is no better," he exclaimed in an anxious tone to a subordinate.

"He is dying," replied Pereco. "He wishes the presence of Father Anselmo."

"Dying! well, that's good news, there is some hope of being relieved from this cursed post. The news will be worth a captaincy, at least, at Madrid, and you perhaps, Pereco, will come in for a share in the good luck. Who knows, if they give me a regiment, you may get a troop?"

"But how can the death of the prisoner benefit us, and to whom will it be so much pleasure at Madrid?"

"Hark thee, Pereco, thou hast been a good fellow, and obedient, can I trust thee with a secret?"

The lieutenant made the usual protestations.

"Well, then, come this way beyond the ears of the lazy scoundrels in the guard room. Dost thou know who our prisoner is?"

A shake of the head was the only reply of the wondering Pereco.

"Well, nor I, but I can guess. Hast thou no suspicions?"

"None. Thou forgettest that he came here before I joined you. I always supposed that he is what he is represented to be, an impostor—a pretender to some Portuguese title. Don something or other."

"An impostor! ay, he may be, but why not try him and hang him. They did not think him an impostor in Venice, and my life in it, they do not think him so at Madrid. Why need the King, our master, trouble himself about a mere Portuguese impostor? The Venitians were compelled to turn him out from their city. He went to Padua. The governor of Padua was compelled a second time to drive him forth. He escaped to Tuscany. The duke was compelled to deliver him up to our viceroy at Naples, and three long years imprisonment in the *Castle del Ovo* was enough to expiate any ordinary imposition. But no, his crime was that he wouldn't die, so they thought they would work him to death in the galleys; but in time, they found his sufferings excited too much the sympathies of his fellow prisoners, and he was ordered to be buried alive up here in this old forgotten, delapidated crow's nest. Thinkest thou that a common prisoner would have been thus treated! Thinkest thou that a mere impostor would have been cared for with so much trouble? No, though they tell us so, he is of more consequence than our masters are willing to admit, and his death will lighten a heavy load in the Escurial."

"But who do you suppose him to be?" interrupted Pereco.

"Who! why the king of Portugal—the rightful owner of the crown now worn by his Most Catholic Majesty. But here comes Father Anselmo. Conduct him to the prisoner."

The priest, accompanied by Pereco, descended to the cell of the dying king. The dim lamp threw a flickering, sickly light over the emaciated and prostrate form of the unhappy Don—a form once so graceful and so stalwart,

"Was never seen a vassal mien so noble and so high,"

—the pride of Lusitanian halls—the glory of the lists. A

flash from the flame of life gleamed for a moment from the glazed eye, his lips moved, he essayed to speak. The priest knelt beside the pallet, and bowed his ear to the mouth of the dying monarch. A low, inarticulate murmur, in which the words "Don Sebastian," were alone audible, struck upon his ear. It ceased. The king was dead.

* * * * * *

Thus died the famous and unfortunate Don—far away from his loving and expecting subjects—and under circumstances which have led many to treat with contempt his pretensions to the title. But not with him perished the popular belief in his existence. It grew in strength from year to year, until it became a settled point in the national faith, which has descended in all its force to the present time.

"Do you expect the return of Don Sebastian?" demands the traveller of the passing peasant.

"*Sim, Senhor Don Sebastiao ainda ade voltar.*"

"*Quando?*"

"*Em poco tempo.*"

THE CAPTAIN'S STORY.

"TALKING of circumstantial evidence, I can tell you a story, in point, of an affair that happened within my own personal knowledge, if you wish to hear it."

The speaker was one of a group that stood upon the promenade-deck of the Empire, one day two or three summers ago, as she glided among the glories of the Hudson, on her downward passage from the political capital of the state to the commercial and financial capital of the Union. This group had been collected by an animated discussion between two professional-looking disputants, respecting the necessity and propriety of killing men as a punishment for murder. The members of it were apparently all strangers to each other, and to the disputants, one of whom, from his appearance in general, and his white cravat in particular, and from his frequent quotations from Scripture—his constant iteration of such phrases as "divine vengeance," "holy indignation," "God's immutable laws," &c. his wordy rhetoric, false logic, and bad temper, I took to be of that small class of narrow-minded and short-sighted religionists who are ever ready to brand reform with the reproach of infidelity; who fancy an earthquake endangering the foundations of God's church in every step of human improvement—who look upon every discovery in science as an attack upon Moses —every new moral maxim as an insult to Solomon—every philanthropic movement as a contempt of our Saviour; a class who seem to think the very drivel and slaver of the pilgrims essential to the existence of the shrine; and who, by this sort of nasty conservatism, do more harm the cause of religion than all the infidels in the world: more harm than their liberal and enlightened brethren of the cloth are able to counteract.

The conversation, at first so spirited as to excite the interest and attention of a number of ladies, who had moved themselves up so as to be within hearing, had begun to flag. The arguments for and against had been pretty nearly exhausted, and the combatants were beginning, in the lull of the battle, to draw off their polemical cohorts, preparatory to a peace, both parties satisfied with the *uti possidetis*, although the spectators could distinguish no great difference between it and the *statu quo ante bellum*.

It was at this opportune moment that the speaker, a square-built, red-faced, comfortable-looking man, proposed to tell his story. Of course, there was a general expression of assent; so clearing his throat with a preparatory "hem," and stowing his quid a little more compactly, after shifting it from starboard to larboard, he began:

"I am a sailor, or rather was, for it is a good many years since I gave up ploughing the deep and took to turning furrows upon the land. Just forty years ago I was in command of a little full-rigged brig, called the Moresco, belonging to Baltimore. We were bound for Liverpool, and from there to the Cape de Verds, for a cargo of salt, and thence home. My crew consisted of three men and a boy—rather short handed you may think for a long voyage; but sailors were in demand, and my vessel was a little bit of a thing, and required but few to manage her; besides, I was young then, and felt myself about equal to the watch of a small frigate alone; and in addition there was the mate, who had come on board of me with the reputation of being as active an officer as ever stepped across a ship's gangway. Mr. Clark—James C. Clark, I think, was his name—was a young man about thirty, but he had been to sea pretty much all his life. Report said, for I didn't know much of him personally, that he was a good sailor, but a regular marine Tartar; a thorough-going disciple of the 'Hell-afloat system.'"

Here there was a movement of increased interest, especially among the ladies; and one of the gentlemen embodying the curiosity of the auditors, demanded of the captain an explanation of the principles of the system he had mentioned.

"It is a system," replied the captain, "much in vogue formerly, and which, I am sorry to say, has not been entirely done away with to this day. It is a system, the fundamental principle of which is, that a sailor—I mean a regular ''fore-the mast' duff-eater, a real 'Jack-nasty face' —is the incarnation of human depravity; that, as the phrase is, 'the better you try to serve him, the worse he tries to serve you;' and that it is necessary to continually work him, and curse him, and flog him, to make him earn the salt-junk and rusty pork upon which he is half-starved."

"But, surely," exclaimed another of the listening group, "such a system can find no advocate in the American service in the present day?"

The captain turned to the speaker, and deliberately eyed him with a peculiarly benign expression, rendered somewhat quizzical by a slight pursing of the lips.

"You believe," at last exclaimed the captain, "in the progress of humanity; in the march of mind; in the development of the genius of American civilization—don't you? Well, it is a comfortable belief; but if you want to keep it, never go to sea before the mast: if you do, ten chances to one you will have it knocked out of you with a marling-spike or a belaying-pin, as soon as your officers get you into blue water. I am sorry to say it; but I have seen things at sea that, if told on shore, would make even the judges of the Marine Court stare; and I have pretty good reason to know that Jack has, to this day, occasional opportunities of seeing some of the 'Devil's doings' when he can't help it. But I'm going rather 'large:' so you see, I'll just board my jawing-tacks, and brace sharp up to my story.

"This Mr. Clark, as I was mentioning, had the reputation of being a good sailor and an active officer; but it was said that he never could get a crew to sail with him the second time, and that more than once he had to secrete himself while his ship was in port, and join her only at the last moment, in order to avoid arrest at the complaint of some of his misused men. But so far from this being against him, there were not a few old sea dogs who really thought that it was in his favor; and even I, at that time, had no very clear idea of the distinction between a good officer and a hard one. Glad, at any rate, was I when Mr. Clark joined the brig, and commenced helping to stow the cargo. I soon found that report had not belied his character, and that he was a thorough driving fellow, who knew what work meant, and how to have it done. He was evidently disposed to severity, with cartmen, stevedores, and others; but I could perceive no evidences of capriciousness or downright bad temper.

"In a few days, owing mainly to his activity and energy, the cargo was aboard and stowed, and the brig ready for sea. Our crew consisting, as I have said, of three men and a boy, came on board; and the wind shifting immediately to 'free,' we 'sheeted-home' every thing, and stood out to sea.

"We had been out but a very few days when I became convinced that Mr. Clark's manner was, to the full, as rough as I had heard it represented. Hardly an order came from his lips unaccompanied by an oath, or some opprobrious epithet. And but little less liberal was he in the use of blows. Upon several occasions I remonstrated with him, but he pleaded so strongly in justification, the necessity of the case, that I was compelled to let him have his way. It is always a delicate thing for a captain to meddle with a mate's authority: discipline is the main point, and upon any disagreement in the cabin it is sure to suffer.

"Another reason for my indisposition to interfere with the exercise of Mr. Clark, of his authority in his own way, was the fact that his displays of bad temper were not wholly unprovoked. Had I had Job himself for first officer, sure I am that his well-tried patience would hardly have enabled him to resist the temptation of flourishing a rope's end, at least a dozen times a day. I was frequently provoked beyond all bounds by the conduct of the men.

"For a small crew, hardly a worse one could have been selected. One of the three men was willing enough, but he was slow and stupid. The others were smart, active fellows, but real grumbling, growling rascals, who had made up their minds, from the first, never to lift a hand or stir a foot when they could help it. They had both been in the English service; and although Americans, they had acquired all the vices of the English sailor. In fact, I recollect that one of them told me that he had made three voyages in a Canadian-timber ship, where, every time they reefed topsails, the officers were compelled to chase the men up the rigging with handspikes.

"To these two men, whose names were the usual sailor-hailing handles, Jack and Bill, the mate had taken a supreme dislike, and they to him. At last things got to be so bad, that not an order of his did they pretend to obey, unless it was accompanied with a curse and a blow; and not unfrequently, in the night, during the mate's watch, when only three persons were on deck, have I been aroused from sleep by the sound of a rope's end on Bill's back, and his yells of rage and pain.

"Well, in this way, cursing and grumbling, and flogging, as thousands of vessels have done since, we made our course across the Atlantic. Had I known as much then as I do now, things would have been different. I would have resolutely set my face against Mr. Clark's brutal and badgering ways on the one hand, and, on the other, I would have triced up Mr. Bill or Jack to the rigging upon the first sufficient provocation, given them three dozen with the cats, in regular man-o'-war style, called the accounts square, and treated them mildly until they had run up another score, to be wiped off in the same way. They would soon have understood how the land lay, and have come to the conclusion that it was time to luff up a bit, and leave off backing and filling round mutiny point. There never was a sailor who would not knock under to a due mixture of severity and kindness; but this constant hectoring only makes him feel bad, and disposes him to run his head against a marling-spike or a belaying-pin, whenever he sees his tormentor have it in hand. However, I was young then, as I have said, and didn't know as much as I do now.

"We left Liverpool; and if it was bad before we got there, it was much worse after we left. Often and often I wished the voyage over, and that Clark and his two bass-drums, as he used to call them, were paid off, and discharged. Generally I enjoy the sea; it is such a grand place for sentiment. I like to come on deck, and after giving an extra pull or two upon the halyards and braces, to walk up and down, and study the ceaseless play of light upon the curling, hissing hills of water. I love to stretch myself upon the booby-hatch or hen-coop, and gaze up into the clear blue vault of heaven, until the stars show themselves in the daylight; and you don't so much as say thankye, but look right past them, up, up to the pure sapphire, where no sunbeams are needed—where God lives, and hosts of angels float in his breath around his Eternal

Throne. I love to lean over the taffrail, and lower my soul out like a deep sea lead, down, down into the fathomless caves of the ocean! I love all this kind of thing, and enjoy myself very much; not that I suppose that my imagination is up to the flights of many of our great American poets; or that I can feel the sentiment of the situation as fully even as many a seasick girl on her first voyage; but still I love to indulge myself, as far as my slender gifts in the sentimental line will permit; and, as I said, generally I enjoy myself at sea very much. But this voyage was an exception—I could neither read, sleep, nor think; and as for anything like a quiet communion with nature, it was out of the question in such a perfect marine pandemonium as the Moresco.

"In three weeks we reached Mayo, the island to which we were bound, and anchored in the roadstead. While getting in our cargo of salt, which took us about two weeks, things went on rather more quietly; but it was only a lull before the storm. Two days out from Mayo, our third man fell sick, and was compelled to keep his berth. This reduced the mate's watch to himself and Bill, while my watch was composed of Jack and the boy.

"It was in the mate's middle watch, on the fourth night after we had started for home, that I was aroused by the usual sounds of Mr. Clark's voice, in tones of high passion. I heard him exclaim, with an oath, 'I'll have your life, you villian! I'll murder you!' and then followed a torrent of imprecations. To this some muttered reply was made, which, as I was almost half asleep at the moment, I could not understand; and then came a quick, heavy tread of feet on deck. 'D——n you,' exclaimed the mate, 'I'll cut your heart out. And then I heard a noise of scuffling—a choking sound—a crashing blow, and the fall of a body on deck.

"At this moment I was sensible, from the motion of the brig, that she was rapidly falling off from the wind; and fearing that she would come round by the lee and be taken aback, I jumped from my berth, and while slipping on my clothes, I shouted to Mr. Clark to mind his helm; but he made no answer.

"I stopped only for my trousers and pea-jacket, and hurried up. As I emerged from the companion-way, I heard a heavy splash in the water, over the starboard-quarter, and I saw Mr. Clark leaning over the bulwark, and with one hand holding on by the maintopmast breast backstay.

"As I stepped towards him he turned, and a flash from the binnacle lamp lighted up his countenance; its expression was awful—a look of horror and fear was rapidly chasing from his features the grin of rage and the flush of physical exertion.

"'Lower away the boat!' he suddenly shouted, in

accents of the wildest agony; 'lower away the boat, quick, quick—Bill has jumped overboard: save him, for God's sake!'

"'Hold!' I exclaimed, 'belay that,' as Mr. Clark jumped to the taffrail, and began to cast off the boat-falls.

"'Into the boat! quick, into the boat!' shouted the mate, in a hoarse and convulsed tone.

"'Stop, Mr. Clarke,' said I, laying my hand upon his shoulder, and drawing him back from the taffrail. 'What shall we man the boat for?'

"'For Bill—Bill is overboard—he jumped overboard!'

"'If Bill is overboard,' interposed Jack, in a surly tone, 'it's the best place for him, I guess: look at this.' And Jack stretched out his hand in the binnacle light.

"'Blood! how is that?'

"'Why, here on deck—and see, you can feel it on the quarter-rail; and here is some hair mixed with it. Bill's hair, by G——!' exclaimed Jack, holding a lock of bloody hair in the light of the galley-lantern, which the old wooden-legged black cook now brought forward.

"'And see here, here is his knife, all covered with blood: I heard Clark ask him for it not ten minutes since.

"'Mr. Clark,' continued Jack, sideling up to the

mate, with a most truculent and lowering visage and tone, 'you'll swing for this, if there is any law in the land. I heard him cry murder, and I've heard you threaten to take his life more than once.'

"'Man the boat! man the boat!' shrieked the mate, wringing his hands, and frantically grasping the boat-falls.

"At this moment it occurred to me that perhaps the sailor might have been merely wounded; and although the chance of picking him up was so small, it was worth the attempt, if only for the mate's sake. So, directing the boy to hoist a lantern in the rigging, while the old cook was to mind the helm, and keep the brig aback, the boat was lowered, and jumping into it with Jack and the mate, I pushed off. With such convulsive strength did Mr. Clark bend his oar, that I had to direct the whole force of the rudder against him, to keep him from pulling Jack round-and-round. Stoutly we rowed out in the blackness to leeward, till the light in the distant brig shone like a fixed star, so small the parallax, or change in the angle of vision, as it rose and fell upon the undulating sea. Frequently we stopped and listened; and frequently the mate's agonizing voice went over the hissing waste of waters, but no groan of the dying came back in reply.

"'There's not much use in this work,' exclaimed Jack.

"I knew that he spoke the truth; and after two

hours' hard pulling I sternly silenced Mr. Clark's remonstrances, and ordered the boat back to the brig. As we mounted to the deck, the purplish light of dawn streamed across the water. The murderer turned his ghastly face towards me, and, in a half-inquiring tone, exclaimed, 'He jumped overboard.' I looked him steadily in the eye for a moment, and deliberately shook my head. His lips became of a bluish-white; his breath seemed to fail him; and staggering forward, he threw himself across the companion-hatch and sobbed violently. The stern, hard man was all gone.

"All day he sat in the cabin upon the transom, with his head bowed upon his hands. I left him the cabin pretty much to himself; but I could not help, as I walked the deck, taking an occasional glance at him through the skylight. In the afternoon he roused himself a little, took a look out of the cabin-windows, got out his desk, and wrote steadily for an hour; and superscribing several letters, directed one of them in words, that, in the distance, looked very much like my name. This was suspicious. I saw that he had made up his mind to something. What was it? What could it be but suicide. It was clearly my duty to prevent this, or at any rate to give him a longer time to think about it; so just at sunset I called Jack and the boy, and went down into the cabin. I at once addressed myself to the criminal, told him plainly my suspicions; told him that

I knew he intended to throw himself overboard; and that as I was determined he should do no such thing, at least for the present, I had come to the resolution of putting him in irons. He started, appeared for the moment somewhat astonished, but readily submitted without saying a word.

"The next morning we were spoken by a brig, which proved to be a United States man-of-war, five days out from Porta Prayo, in the island of St. Jago, and bound for the Chesapeake. The first lieutenant came aboard of us, and after hearing my story, took me back with him to see his captain, who decided at once to transfer Mr. Clark to his vessel, and carry him home for trial. At the same time he loaned me three active fellows, to supply his place; without which I could not have got along at all, seeing that my third man was likely to be, for some time, confined to his berth. When all was arranged, we filled-away, and stood on in company—both being bound for the capes of the Chesapeake. The man-of-war, however, outsailed us; and it was not until a week after her arrival that I got in with the Moresco. In the meantime Mr. Clarke had been handed over to those who had jurisdiction on shore; and as soon as we arrived, all hands were ordered up as witnesses, and preparations for his trial at once commenced. Somehow or another they were not so long about such kind of things then as now. The lawyers were not so expert in staving off cases and bamboozling judges; and the juries just as leave hang a man as look at him, if he had fairly thrust his head in the noose. There has been a change since then; whether for the better or worse, I can't say—but I suppose for the better. The truth is, I've seen so many changes, which in the beginning I have been a little dubious about, turn out so well in the end, that I'm determined never to say anything new is wrong again. Why, I've seen the time when I've thought that a ship was no ship unless her shrouds were cat-harpened in as tightly as the ribs of a Broadway belle. I've turned up my nose at chain-cables, and d——d the lubber's eyes who first dared to lead the maintopmast stay anywhere else than to the head of the foremast; but if I was at anchor on rocky ground, off a lee-shore, wouldn't I like to have iron ground-tackle to hang by? or if a heavy lurch whipped out my foremast, wouldn't I be glad that my maintopmast stay wasn't fastened to the head of it? No, no, the world is not so perfect yet that one could wish it to stand still. There are catharpens on the shrouds of society that would be well to get rid of; and there are many improvements in the mode of setting up and rattling down the standing-rigging; why, it is only within a short time that it has been found that the great national ark carries her spars easier when you slacken the stays; and that in working to windward, you must not round-in the lee braces too taut, or what you make up in pointing, you'll lose in going ahead.

"Well, well," continued the captain to his auditors, "I see that you think that I am going rather large; but just wait a minute till I put my helm down, and brace up again once more, and I'll weather the whole story in half the shake of a shark's tail.

"It is not necessary to go into a long account of the trial. Suffice it to say, that my evidence, light as I could make it, was heavy against the prisoner. I was compelled to testify to the bad blood between him and the dead man—the words and sounds I heard that night—the splash in the water—the attitude of Clark over the bulwark—the blood and hair found on the deck and rail. But if my evidence was hard, Jack's was still harder: he swore that the mate had told him, two or three times, that he, the mate, 'would have Bill's life.' He swore that, not more than ten minutes before the row, he heard Mr. Clark ask Bill for his sheath-knife; that shortly, after he heard the mate say, 'D—n you, I'll murder you;' that there was scuffling, and the sound of two or three blows, and a cry of murder, to which he should have paid no attention, had it not been for the low and peculiar tone in which it was uttered; that upon this, he sprung upon the deck, and saw the mate in the very act of lifting the body over the quarter-bulwark.

"The evidence of the sick man, boy, and cook, was all, as far as it went, to the same effect: and by the time it was all in, it was all up with Mr. Clark—he didn't need a long speech from the district attorney to finish him; without that, he stood no more chance for his life than a flying-fish does among a school of dolphins. The jury brought him in guilty, after about fifteen minutes' deliberation; and next day the judge sentenced him to be hanged."

"And was he hanged?" demanded one of the group of listeners, as the captain paused in his story.

"Certainly," replied the captain; "they put a rope around his neck, and, knocking out the platform from beneath him, left him dancing the pirate's jig upon nothing. He kicked and struggled for a long time; but I suppose that made the sight more instructive—a greater moral lesson. Oh! he was hanged by the neck until he was dead; for I saw the body afterwards."

"And it served him right," exclaimed the gentleman who had been the advocate of capital punishment in the recent dispute—"served him right; it was a clear case of murder."

"Yes, it was a clear case—a very clear case; and yet, to my certain knowledge, there was no murder about it."

"How so?" exclaimed a dozen voices. "Do you think that he did not mean to kill the sailor?"

"I don't think at all; I know. I know not only that he did not mean to kill the man, but that no man was killed."

An expression of increased interest now escaped the group, which gathered up closer around the narrator.

"Listen," he continued, "and I'll just reel off my yarn, and whip the fag-end of it in half a minute.

"It was about five years afterwards that I took a cargo of tobacco to Gibraltar, to supply the *contrabandistas*, who under the broad and powerful shield of the English flag, make the Rock a depot for goods to be smuggled into Spain. Well, I was ashore one day, attending the sale of some goods at auction in Commercial Square, when, among the sailors who were loitering about, I saw one whose face struck me as being very familiar, but whose name I could not recollect. He passed on; and I should have thought no more about it, such things being common enough, had there not been something in the fellow's look that struck me as being very peculiar, and induced me to pause and think where I had seen him. Suddenly a recollection of the Moresco business came over me like a blaze of sheet lightning in a dark night. 'That's either Bill, Bill's twin-brother, his ghost, or the devil,' said I, as I jumped from a tobacco hogshead, and almost knocked down the American Consul, and fairly running over two Moors, three Jews, and a jackass, took after the sailor. who was still in sight. As I came up with him, he turned, and I could see at once that he recognised me. He touched his tarpaulin, took my offered hand, and called me by name; there could be no doubt that he was the identical Bill.

" 'I suppose, captain,' said he, 'that you thought that I had gone to Davy Jones' long ago; but you see I'm alive and flapping. How have you been this long time? How is my old friend, Mr. Clarke?'

" 'Mr. Clark!' said I, 'Mr. Clarke was hanged!'

" 'Hanged! the d—l! why that's worse luck than I ever wished him. I only expected that his watch would pitch him overboard some dark night. But what was he hanged for?'

" 'For murdering you.'

" 'For murdering me!' exclaimed Bill, in astonishment; and I had to repeat the assertion, with an account of the whole affair, to convince him of its truth. 'And now,' said I, 'how is it that I see you alive?'

"We walked out upon the bastion, and took a seat upon the banquette, when Bill began his story; which it would be tiresome to tell in his words. The amount of it was, that he had frequently threatened Mr. Clark that he would jump overboard, and that he had nearly made up his mind several times to do so; that he came on deck that night, feeling sore from a recent flogging, and somewhat excited by drink, which he and Jack had bribed the old cook to steal from the cabin; that for some time Mr. Clarke had the helm, and that after asking for his knife and returning it again, Mr. Clark ordered him to take the wheel; to which he, Bill, replied that it was not his turn yet, and that he, the mate, might lash it or leave it, and be d—ned. Upon this the row commenced. Mr. Clark jumped at him, struck him a blow in the face, and knocked him down; and that, in falling, his knife came out of the sheath, and, getting under him, inflicted a wound in his side; that, as soon as he could get upon his feet, maddened by rage, pain, and drink, and reckless of life, but anxious to spite Mr. Clark, he had jumped upon the bulwark, resolved to throw himself into the sea; that Mr. Clark seized him, and endeavored to drag him on board; and that it was Mr. Clark's voice that cried for help. With a sudden effort Bill tore from the mate's grasp, and sank into the water. In falling, he struck his head in the main chains, and for a long time was insensible. Upon coming to himself, the love of life returned, and induced him to exert his powers as a swimmer to sustain himself upon the surface. He kept up until just at daylight, when, his strength being quite spent, he saw a large ship bearing down upon him. She came so close as to hear his feeble hail; and lowering a boat, picked him up and took him on board, where rest and kind nursing soon restored him to strength. The wound in his side was slight, and healed up completely before the ship reached Liverpool. Since that time Bill had been knocking about the world from various ports, until at last his luck had brought him to Gibraltar; and there he stood before me, a living proof of the fallibility of human testimony, and the danger of relying upon circumstantial evidence.

"'I don't want to see any more hanging matches,' said the captain, after a pause, drawing a piece of cavendish from his pocket, and politely tendering it to his auditors, 'I don't want to see any more great moral lessons preached from the gallows or the yard-arm.' And twisting off a piece of the dainty weed, the captain marched off, with the conscious air that always marks your habitual *raconteur*, when he thinks that he has told a story in point."

WASHINGTON'S

FIRST BATTLE;

OR

BRADDOCK'S DEFEAT.

"Ho! stranger, halt! which way so late?"
Loud shouts a woodman bold:
"The day's short race is nearly run,
The nights are dark and cold;
The forest lies on either hand;
The prairie rolls before;
And strangers ne'er do I permit
To pass my cabin-door."

The ruddy fire, with cheerful glow,
Salutes the stranger's sight,
And throws, in bright and joyous gleams,
Around its mellow light,
On blackened walls, from which depend
The spoils of many a chase,
On horns, and hides, and antlers broad,
That beams and rafters grace.

In Sparks' Biography of Washington it is stated that there were living, a few years since, at least two men who had been in this battle.

On flesh of buffalo and bear—
  The hump—the sav'ry tongue—
The ven'son haunch, and feathered game,
  Which round the room are hung;
The well-oiled rifles o'er the fire,
  Enwrapped in doe-skin case,
And 'neath a *Pater Patriæ*,
  With grave, majestic face.

Within the chimney's ample jaws,
  Which near across one side,
Insatiate with a forest's spoil,
  Yawn deep, and high, and wide;
There sits a shrunk and withered form,
  A doting, white-haired sire—
His palsied frame rejoicing in
  The warm and genial fire.

Across his knees a rifle rests,
  That worn, and stained, and bent,
And marked with many a seamy scar,
  And many a deep indent,
He fondles, child-like, and the while,
  With trembling hands, counts o'er
A row of notches on the stock,
  Which number just three-score.

Three-score in full the notches count;
Again he runs them o'er,
Again he shakes his snowy head,
And murmurs—"There were more."
Now, pausing at the stranger's voice,
He lifts his dim, blear eyes:
The words unmeaning strike his ear—
He turns away, and sighs.

"The Chippewah and Mingo fierce,
The proud and bold Shennoah,
The Rundak, and the Ottawah—
I'm sure that there were more!"
The woodsman marks the furtive glance
That by his guest is cast:
"He's very old," he prompt replies,
"His mind is failing fast.

"A hundred winters' snows and winds
Have bleached his hairs so white;
A hundred summers' lights and shades
Have dimn'd his eagle sight;
Now bowed, and shrunk with weight of years,
There's little to recall
The ranger bold, the hunter keen,
So lithe, and strong, and tall.

"Ere Lexington's far-echoing guns
Had thrilled each patriot heart,
And heralded the glorious war
In which he bore a part,
Amongst our French and Indian foes
He'd won a fear-fraught name;
And throughout all the border woods
That rifle shared his fame.

"Those notches marked upon the stock,
A fearful story tell
Of scores of ruthless savage fiends
Who 'fore its flashes fell;
Its sure and fatal bullets were
With death's own signet sealed;
While oft that tomahawk and knife
Have lighted up in foremost strife
The darkest battle-field.

"But now adown his stirring life's
Prolonged, eventful track,
Forgetting all his latter deeds,
His mem'ry travels back;
And as when rivulet we trace,
By springs pellucid fed,
More pure and bright the waters flow
When near the fountain-head—

"So, as his mind thus backward glides,
  Along life's flowing streams,
The scenes of youth, most bright and clear,
  Float through his waking dreams—
Ohio's dark and bloody fork!
  Otsego's hill-crowned shore,
The Ca-na-wa-ga's broad, pure stream,
  The vale of Shenandoah."

While thus the hardy woodsman spake,
  His wife and daughters fair,
The hospitable evening meal
  With bustling haste prepare;
And now from embers glowing red,
  A sav'ry steam ascends,
That to the toil-won appetite
  A keener vigor lends.

Now deaftly is the groaning board
  With food profusely spread—
The haunch, the hump, the fat bear's steak,
  The smoking, hot, maize bread.
While soon by all around the board
  Is felt the satiate glow;
They raise their heads, the tide of talk
  Resumes its cheerful flow.

The question free, the frank reply,
The scenes of western life,
The lucky shot, the desperate race,
The daring leap, the adventurous chase,
And deeds of blood and strife.
The stranger, too, has tales to tell
Of far off eastern lands,
To which the good wife's heart is linked
By mem'ry's golden bands.

" 'Tis where 'Gahela pours his flood,"
To her demand he cries,
But instantly his words are checked—
He turns with vague surprise;
For, lightly bounding to his feet,
That poor old dotard springs,
And crashing on the stony hearth,
His rifle rudely rings.

The barrel of the battered piece
One hand, now steady, clasps;
The other, firm and nervously
The stranger's shoulder grasps:
"Monongahela! dost thou say?
Monongahela's flood!
Ah! tell me, if it blushes still,
If still its stream runs blood!"

"Ah, no! ah, no! I quite forget;—
'Tis seventy years, and more,
Since by these eyes was seen that sight—
That sight so sad and sore;
And yet, it seems as 'twere to-day,
So fiercely on my brain
The visions rush of that sad hour,
That wild and gory plain."

"I see the proud and gaudy ranks,
'Gahela gleaming bright;
I see the march, the fight, the foe,
And, ah! that shameful flight."

The old man on his rifle leans,
His voice comes loud and clear;
"List, list," he cries, "while I recount
That tale of blood and fear."

* * * *

"Ho! news, great news! Provincials bold,
Ho! sound the fife and drums,
To guard us from the savage foe,
The gallant Braddock comes!
Ho! news, great news, Provincials bold!
Across the ocean wave,
Two regiments the king has sent,
Our hearths and homes to save!

"Hurrah! Provincials, shout hurrah!
Raise high the bonfire light!
Two regiments of royal troops,
To teach us how to fight!
Denwiddie, Sherley, and old Sharp,
Have planned the whole campaign—
Hurrah! hurrah! we'll strain our throats
For captured Fort Duquesne!

"Of full five hundred royal troops
Sir Peter* rides the head;
Another corps of equal strength
By bold Dunbar is led;
Meanwhile, in garrisons and camps,
And through the country round,
Another full five hundred troops,
Right royal troops, are found.

"Peyrouny's rangers swell the train
With Poulson's rifle corps;
While from the North young gallant Gates
Brings up scarce quite a score—
A few poor, plain, Provincial troops,
All useless in the fight,
But privileg'd to look upon
This show of British might!!

* Sir Peter Halket.

"And now abroad, its flaunting folds
Each banner proudly flings;
With new and unaccustomed sounds
The western forest rings;
The pomp of trumpet, fife and drum,
The tramp—the clash of steel—
The lumbering artillery—
The cason's groaning wheel—

"The deeply-laden baggage wains—
A long, far-stretching train,
That slowly winds its untracked way
Through forest, swamp, and plain;
With shouts, and songs, and noisy cheers,
And loud-resounding blows,
Which fiercely on his straining team
Each driver free bestows.

"The sturdy giants of the wood,
In vernal foilage crowned,
As if amazed, in wond'ring tones
Repeat each novel sound;
While listening to the careless din,
The wary Indian scout,
By ear alone, unheard, unseen,
Marks well our devious route.

"At length, with weary months of toil,
Our destined post we near:
The van with Braddock pushes on—
Dunbar brings up the rear;
At head of twice six hundred men,
Sparks, Gage, and Halket ride,
Where joins with Yougheogany
Monongahela's tide.

"There, turning from the rugged hills
That skirt the northern banks,
Across Monongahela's ford
They lead the glit'ring ranks;
And wheel along the level shore,
Where opes a lengthened glade,
Upon the sun-lit river's brink,
And 'neath the forest's shade.

"Oh, ne'er was seen more gallant sight,
As burst the orb of day
On that long line of stately troops,
In all their proud array;*
The polished casques—the waving plumes,
The muskets burnished bright,
Far flashing through the open wood
The level beams of light.

* Washington, in one of his letters, says that he never saw a more gallant military show than was presented by these troops when he joined them, after first crossing the Monongahela.

"But who is this upon our track,
Who, here with flowing rein,
Comes spurring with impatient speed,
Our column's front to gain?
Though fever's rage has paled his cheek,
And sunk his flashing eye,
His stalwart form still towers with pride—
His mein is firm and high.

"On him the proud Provincials all
Turn looks of pleased surprise,
And greet him to the field once more
With smiles and beaming eyes;
And well they may, for well they know
Virginia's gallant son—
The peerless horseman, soldier, chief,
The youthful Washington.

"And now again we cross the stream,
The northern bank regain,
And rising from the river's bed,
Ascend an open plain;
That smiling plain, so quiet, smooth,
With woods environed round,
And over at its farthest verge
With gentle hillocks crowned—

"Embosomed in the forest dark,
And clothed in richest green,
It softly woos the bright sunbeams,
And glows in summer sheen,
A dimple in wild nature's cheek,
Refining features rude,
And lighting up with joyant smile
The forest's solitude.

"And thus it lay, so bright and still,
With not a sound of life,
Save voice of one ill-omened bird,
Who, prescient of the strife,
Surveys our noisy, gallant show—
Surveys our still and ambushed foe,
From perch far over head,
And loudly calls his sable kin
To banquet on the dead.

"Once more in vain 'tis strongly urged,
That some Provincial corps
Of scouts, trained up to Indian wiles,
The woods around explore;
But Braddock no advice will hear,
No ambush does he dread—
'Who'll dare confront a British force
While *he* is at its head?'

"With ranks compact, our stately troops
Tramp o'er the grass-grown plain;
Hurrah! we'll march for three short leagues,
And rest in doomed Duquesne;
With ranks compact, and steady steps,
Hearts beating high with hope,
Our gleaming columns foremost files
Ascend the gentle slope.

"Crash! crash! from out the very ground,
Up which our front ranks wheel,
Shoots forth a sheet of livid flame—
They falter, stagger, reel;
In front, on flank, the furious blast
Pours forth from deep ravine,
Where, covered by the tall rank grass,
No mortal foe is seen.

"As when, unheralded by sign,
The thunder-storm awakes
The slumb'ring wood, and far and wide
The dreamy silence breaks;
As when no cloud forshades the bolt,
But 'mid its startling crash,
Upon the leaves the big drops fall
With deep and sullen plash.

"So breaks that wild and deadly storm,
So roars that deadly blast,
So sullen on defenceless breasts
The leaden drops fall fast.
A moment's pause! Again it comes
In one continuous shower,
And from each tree, and bush, and tuft,
The murky flashes lower.

"A thousand rifles flashing fast,
Dispatch with sulphu'rous breath,
From 'neath the covers, dark and dense,
Their messengers of death;
A thousand rifles flashing fast,
The angry echoes wake,
And joined with shouts, and oaths and yells,
Wild, hellish music make.

"Rash Gage's corps, which forms our van,
Dismayed, with looks aghast,
Rush back, and our advancing ranks
In deep disorder cast.
The panic spreads—confused, deranged,
And paralyzed with fear,
No orders will the dastards mind,
No leaders will they hear.

"'To cover! take to cover, men!'
Peyrouny fiercely shouts;
'Beneath the wood, creep on their flank,
My brave and vet'ran scouts!'
'To cover! take to cover men!'
Bold Poulson's voice replies;
'Stir not, stir not, stand fast and firm!'
Besotted Braddock cries.

"'Deploy, deploy, wheel into line,
Advance the serried rank;
From covert foe 't shall ne'er be said
A British soldier shrank!'
Bold, but besotted Braddock, hold!
Alas! he little knows
What cowards he to battle leads,
What 'vantage has his foes.

"Amid the fierce, death-dealing storm,
Athwart the field he flies,
And vainly his poor quailing troops
To form and rally tries;
And vainly Orme, and Washington,
His aids, with orders ride;
The bloody rowels striking deep
The panting courser's side.

"'One gallant charge!' Sir Peter cries;
'Hurrah! who follows me?
Before one firm, determined charge
The skulking foe will flee.'
And at the word, unto a man,
The fearless leaders spring,
And round their heads invitingly
Their flashing sabres swing.

"Five times those gallant, dauntless men
Rush on that line of fire—
Five times before its hissing flames
With thinned ranks retire;
And every time, with gesture, voice,
Entreaties, hoarse commands,
They strive to lead up to the charge
Their panic-stricken bands.

"In vain! no cheers will urge them on,
No words their ranks restore,
But mid their own brave officers
Their aimless volleys pour;
And as around their fellows fall,
Those trained and showy troops
Rush to and fro across the field
In wild, tumultuous groups.

"'Now curses on the dastard fools!'
Peyrouny fiercely cries;
A rifle bullet through his heart—
He staggers, falls, and dies.
Five horses under him shot down,
A British ball, ('tis said,)
Bold Braddock wounded, lays alow,
With Shirley, Halket, dead.

"Morris, and Orme, and Gage are down,
With Sparks and brave St. Clair,
And Burton, too, with many more,
The same hard fate doth share.
As fiercest on the tallest trees
Is poured the lightning's wrath,
So fiercest by the plume-marked brave
Is felt the death-storm's scath—

"'Till not a mounted chief remains,
Save one—that only one,
Who coolly rides 'midst smoke and flame,
The gallant Washington.
Alone, of all that field, he rides,
Majestic, calm, serene—
The noblest target that by foe
In battle e'er was seen.

"Alone, of all that field, he rides,
A mark for every eye,
Round which the spiteful bullets hiss,
Like adders in the sky;
And as from point to point he moves
Unharmed, demoniac cries
From wond'ring and infuriate foes
With ten-fold fury rise.

"Twice 'neath him have his steeds gone down
Before the leaden sleet—
No lack of empty saddles there,
He instant vaults to seat;
And scathless, freely dashes through
The thickest of the strife;
Till e'en the savages respect
His heaven-protected life.

"Six times a chief his rifle points
Against his manly breast,
With careful and delib'rate sight,
And firm and steady rest;
Six times at that same noble mark
His Braves aim fair and nigh—
Six times the hissing volleys pass
The hero harmless by.

"'Desist! desist!' the chieftain cries;
'I see the Spirit's arm
Outstretched, that lofty form to save
And shield from every harm.
For some high duty he's reserved,
Some purpose to fulfil,
And wrong and vain 'twill be to strive
God's chosen one to kill.'

"'Extend your lines, Virginians,
Stretch out on left and right;
Our duty and our honor 'tis
To shield these cowards' flight.'
Encouraged by his cheerful voice,
We stoutly stand at bay,
And as the fiends from cover leap,
Our rifles steady play.

"Retreating slowly, face to foe,
The river's brink we gain,
But sorely pressed—of all our corps
Scarce thirty men remain.
Ah! what a scene of pain and death,
Defeat, disgrace, distress,
As to the calm, bright river's bed
The frantic soldiers press.

"With pallid cheeks, in fearful haste,
They dash adown the banks,
Where three short hours before upsprang
Their proud and glitt'ring ranks;
Their dripping wounds entinting wide.
As o'er the ford they rush,
Upon the shamed indignant tide
A deep and gory blush.

"And as we cross, what hellish sounds
Rise from that fatal plain,
And swell o'er stream and echoing woods
A wild demoniac strain!
Yells, shouts and shrieks, of man and steed
Wrung forth in pain and fright,
And ruthless deeds of savage rage
'Pall heaving soul and sight.

"Like tigers springing from their lairs,
The red-skins throng the plain,
Where, weltering together, lie
The wounded and the slain:
Like tigers to a feast of blood
They rush upon their prey,
And tear from the unstiffened dead
The reeking scalps away.

"Or worse, the wounded, low, in pain,
Yet still instinct with life,
Feel circling round their death-damp brows
The keen and searing knife;
And, as in agony they writhe,
Beseech with failing breath,
In vain, the yelling fiends to grant
The last, poor boon of death.

"But well for us, the scalps and spoils
The savages detain,
Or not a man had lived to see
Home, wife or child again.
No, not a man bold Dunbar's camp
Had reached, the tale to tell—
How, on that fatal, bloody field
Six hundred soldiers fell;
How British ignorance and pride
Heaped in inglorious grave,
By dark Monongahela's banks,
The coward and the brave."

* * * *

"Ah! stranger, many a fight I've seen,
Full many a bloody fray,
But ever stern hath mem'ry held
The sights I saw that day.

I've seen them in the forest wild,
Beneath the greenwood tree,
And where the prairie rolls its waves—
A boundless, grassy sea.

"In field, and camp, and festive hall,
The long, adventurous chase,
Or tracking like a blood-hound fierce,
The prowling red man's trace,
They've steeled my heart, and fired my blood,
Quickened my pulses beat,
Have aimed the ball, and edged the knife,
Have nerved my arm in hours of strife,
And winged my agile feet.

"But ah! the thirst of vengeance o'er,
Fierce passions quiet sleep;
And much, I fear, my greedy lips
Have quaffed the cup too deep.
Too deep! ah! yes, the vengeful draught
Too deeply have I drained,
And all too deep this aged hand
With red men's blood is stained."

* * * *

The old man stops! his strength is spent,
The flash deserts his eye;

Trembling, he sinks into his seat,
  And heaves a gentle sigh,
And mutters to himself again,
  And shakes his snowy head,
As slowly he counts o'er and o'er
  The Tally of the Dead!

A LEGEND

OF

THE CAPE DE VERDES;

AN OMITTED CHAPTER OF "KALOOLAH."

"It is a curious fact, that at the time of the discovery of the islands, the Peak of Fuego did not exist; that is, if we may believe the traditions of the inhabitants. Certain it is, that Cade Mosto, an adventurous Genoese—in the service of the Portuguese—who discovered them, makes no mention of it; and it was some time after his day that the name he gave it—St. Felipe—was superseded by that of Fuego, or island of fire. It seems, that shortly after Cada Mosto's visit, the whole island was enveloped in flames, and that, in consequence, no efforts were made to people it for many years. At length, the fire having subsided, excepting at what is now the Peak, the king of Portugal issued an edict, granting the lands to whoever would settle upon them; and a scanty population was soon drawn from St. Jago, Mayo, and the other islands—partly allured by the hope of finding some of the gold which, according to tradition, was the cause of the fire.

"Among our crew, as I have said, were several Portuguese, two or three of whom were natives of the Cape de Verdes—black, curly-headed fellows, with marks of the strong infusion of negro blood, common to all the inhabitants of the islands. It was of these, and surrounded by a group of other sailors, that I was making some inquiries in relation to *Fonta de Villa* and the little town of *La Ghate*, off which we were becalmed. All at once a broad glare of light shot up from the dark mountain, illuminating the rugged sides, and streaming in the darkness of the night far out to seaward.

"'El Pico! El Pico!' exclaimed a dozen voices.

"Two tall columns flashed upward from the mountain; at one moment steady and erect—the next, quivering and swaying to and fro in the currents of the wind; now seeming to repel each other, now bowing, crouching and turning, like wary combatants preparing for a struggle for life or death, they would rush at each other, close, and writhe for an instant in the fierce embrace.

"'*Los Padres!*' shouted one fellow. '*Los Magicos!*' exclaimed a second. '*Los Alquimistas!*' bellowed a third.

"'Priests, magicians, and alchemists! What do you mean?' I demanded.

"'Oh, ask Pedro Vosalo,' replied one of the crew; 'he was born just round the point, where you see so many sea-weed fires, in the little bay of *Nossa Senora*, and he knows all about it. Pedro! Pedro! come here, and tell *senor el medico* the story of the magicians.'

"Nothing loth, Master Pedro, a little round-shouldered, bandy-legged mulatto, came forward, and throwing aside the stump of his paper segar, commenced his story, which, fortunately for the reader, I am not disposed to attempt giving in the execrable *patois*, half Spanish and half Portuguese, in which it was told."

The above is an extract from the romance of Kaloolah. While that work was going through the press, it was found necessary, in order to keep it within certain limits as to size and price, to suppress a good many pages. Among matter thus thrown out was Pedro's story, which ran as follows:

"You must know, senor," began Pedro, "that many, many years ago there lived over on the other island of Jago two very celebrated men, who were renowned as much for their knowledge, as for their pretended piety and holiness. They were both monks of the most holy order of St. Dominick. The name of the one was Father Gonzalo, and of the other Father Alvarez. No one knew anything of their history, except that they had been great travellers and students. They had not known each other until their arrival at St. Jago; but they immediately formed a great friendship. They kept aloof from their brethren of the convent, and were often heard talking together in a very queer kind of language, and seen drawing the most diabolical figures upon the ground. Still they were such very good Christians to all appearance, that no one dared to say anything against them openly, although the brethren in time began to think that they knew a great deal more than a pious man ought to, and that they might be wizards, or perhaps alchemists."

"Alchemists!" I demanded. "What do you understand by that?"

"I don't know, senor; but Father Chacon used to tell us that it was something a great deal worse than a witch, or a magician. God save us from all such;" and here the little rascal devoutly crossed himself, in which he was followed by his cut-throat companions who were grouped around us.

"Well, things went on in this way for a long time," continued Pedro, "until at last the two Fathers began to find out that everybody suspected them; and so they resolved to come over to this island and live. At that time it was supposed that there was not a single inhabitant here. There was no Peak then, but it was very high and rocky, and it was covered all over so thick with sulphur, that there was no place where you could plant an olive tree or a grape vine.

"Very glad were the people of St. Jago when the two Fathers took a small boat and set out; because, although they had done no harm to any one, every one was afraid that some day, with their great knowledge, they would destroy the town, and perhaps the whole island. No one could feel safe for a moment when he knew that they had sold their souls, and that at any moment the Evil One might come for them, and perhaps take the opportunity to carry off more than he had bargained for; because you see, senor, the Devil, if he can get an excuse for coming into a town, has a right to carry off any one who has neglected to confess or attend mass."

"Indeed! I was not aware," said I, "that that was a privilege of his Satanic Excellency."

"Oh, yes, senor, I have often heard Father Chacon say so. Well, you see the monks landed and set about building a stone hut, thinking that they were all alone upon the island, when, in the midst of their work, they saw coming towards them a stately, noble, well-dressed cavalier—a real Don. He was dressed in a magnificent cloth cloak, beneath which he wore a shirt of mail, covered in front with a leather apron with slits in it, into which were stuck a huge dagger, and two or three pairs of pistols. The scabbard of his long *spado*, or sword, was made to open by means of a spring, to save time and trouble in drawing the weapon, and over the pummel was hung a chaplet of beads, like a good and Christian gentleman. Upon his head he wore a high peaked hat, with a brim an arm's length in width, and looped up a little on one side with a silk cord and a tassel as big as my fist. Oh! wasn't that a most splendid dress! I've had it described to me fifty times, and it seems to me that I never could get tired of hearing of it."

"Or talking of it either, *Senor hablatesta*," interposed a rough *guardian del contramaestre*, or boatswain's mate. "Go on with your story, and don't stand jabbering about it all night."

Thus admonished, Pedro continued his discourse.

"The Don saluted the two monks, and welcomed them to the island, upon which he said he had been for many years, having been wrecked on his passage to the *Mina*, or Gold-coast, and the only one saved out of the whole crew. He offered them any assistance in his power; and soon the three grew very friendly, each one glad of the new acquaintance he had made.

"In this way they lived together for several days, until at last the Don told the monks, among other things, that there was plenty of gold on the island; and at their request he took them and showed them where it was to be found. As soon as they saw the gold, the monks began to think that their new friend was one too many, and that it would be much better to share the gold between two than three: so they consulted together, and concluded to murder the Don in his sleep. But for my part, I can't see why, if they were great magicians, and could make gold, they should have been so anxious to keep the Don out of his share of what he had found.

"But so it was: they killed the Don, and began collecting the gold which he had shown them. But they had not worked long at that business before they began to disagree. Each one wanted to assume power over the other, and each one expressed a determination to lay claim to more than half the precious metal; so that from being the best of friends they soon came to be mortal foes.

"'I tell you,' said Gonzalo, 'that I am the most renowned and learned magician of the two. Have I not studied in the East at the very fountain-head of science? Have I not been taught the mysteries of the most holy *Cabaa.* Am I not the favorite disciple of my master *Mahmoud?* I tell you I am the superior, and I will be obeyed.'

"'Go to,' replied Alvarez, 'with your *Cabaa* and your *Mahmoud.* Havn't I travelled all over Soudan and Bambarra, and lived in the great city of Tombute, and don't I know all the mysteries of the *Fetish*, and am I not the favorite disciple of the great *Obih?* Go to, I say, I am the most learned and the most powerful magician, and I will be obeyed.'

"And so they wrangled for three days, and then they withdrew to different parts of the island, and commenced working at their art, each one to destroy the other. All kinds of tricks and sorceries and incantations they practised against each other; and the fight between Mahmoud and Obih lasted a great many weeks. All that time the island was covered with thick clouds, which could be plainly seen at St. Jago; and in the clouds hosts of spirits rushed upon one another night and day with a most terrific noise.

"One night the good citizens of Ribeyro Grande were startled by a great light, and looking over this way, they saw the whole island in flames. The magicians had set it on fire"——

"Whether by accident or design is not known, I suppose?"

"No, senor, but Father Chacon used to tell us that the way he thought it came about was this. You see the ground was all covered with sulphur, and one of the magicians used such a powerful charm to call up the Evil Spirit, that he was compelled to come instantly, without time to cool on the way; so that arriving here hissing hot, the moment his fiery feet touched the sulphur the whole soil took fire."

"A very probable supposition of Father Chacon," said I.

"Oh! yes, senor; Father Chacon knows how all such things come about. But to finish my story. The fire continued to burn for a great many years; and amidst the flame and smoke the magicians could be seen fighting with each other, aided by vast armies of spirits and demons."

"And which conquered?"

"Oh! neither of them as yet, senor. They keep it up yet, as you can see with your own eyes. Those two flames are the magicians themselves. You see the gold is in the mountain, and when the fire subsided, and people came over here from the other islands, the two monks took up their residence in the Peak, and by their struggles have raised it up so high Sometimes for weeks you can hear them growling and threatening, and throwing great stones with so much force, that at times they fly up into the sky twice as high as the mountain; and sometimes they come out and fight upon the top of the Peak, as they do to-night. See, now they have got hold of each other, and hear how they bellow and roar."

The flames now rushed together, writhed and twisted, again separated and again united, with an appearance of animosity and rage that might almost justify a belief in the legend.

"And the gold," said I, "has any of it ever been found?"

"No, senor; but the inhabitants are in hopes every day that some of it will be thrown over the side of the mountain. Whenever there is a great eruption they always go to look for it; but as yet they have never found anything but pumice stones and sulphur. Some day it will come, and then won't they be rich? The meanest fisherman of Fonta de Villa will have sombreros with a brim as large as our *bonetas de Foynes,* (jib bonnets,) and cloaks that will come down to their heels, and rosaries of real coral and pearls."

The traveller, whose bad luck it may be to put up at the dirty *posada,* in the little miserable town of *La Ghate,* will find upon inquiry that Pedro's story is a true legend of Fuego, and that the common people are not alone in their belief of its truth. It is a matter of faith as well with the priests, the dignitaries, and the governor of the town, which it would take two or three courses of geological lectures to unsettle. Fortunately for the credit of the wizards of the Peak, there is no lyceum at *La Ghate,* and the schoolmaster has never taken the Cape de Verdes in his tour.

A REAL PIRATE.

In this enlightened age, the notion obtains very extensively that a real, veritable, bona-fide pirate, is quite an obsolete affair—a character of the past—a fellow who has performed his part, and retired from the world's stage for ever, leaving behind him nothing but his name and a few pleasant and poetical associations; among which occur black flags, and bloody, emblazoned with death's heads; scuttled ships, with projecting planks nicely balanced over their quarter rails; and low, black schooners, with masts stepped at an angle of forty-five degrees, or, as the sailors say, "half way between nothing at all and a church-steeple." Talking of pirates, people at once think of the Buccaneers, or the Salle Rovers; and if by special invitation their attention is attracted to the piratical of modern times, they boggle at Lafitte and the victims of Commodore Porter's cruise, and come to a dead halt at the mention of the renowned Wansley and Gibbs. Beyond these two worthies, now some fifteen years defunct, it is almost impossible to coax the credulity of a single member of this not-to-be-humbugged community. No! it's of no use. Then and there, on Bedlow's Island, was hanged until it was dead, the romance of the seas; and now, of all those who go down to the sea in ships, and do their business in the great waters, you can't find a dozen who, apart from the question of Malay proas off the coast of Sumatra and around Java Head, have any more respect for pirates than a modern boy of eight years old has for ghosts or the devil. Alas, for the good old piratical and poetical! both have been swamped in the floods of utilitarianism; often united in their lives, in their deaths they are not divided. In this respect, however, their degenerate progeny may be said to resemble them, but with a difference: the old piratical was always poetical; the new poetical, 'tis said, is often, if not always, piratical.

The piratical having thus nearly disappeared as an element of the social state, and a very general skepticism as to any lingering remnants of it having taken possession of the public mind, it behoves any one about to introduce a real pirate into general society, to preface his appearance by an assertion of his claims to confidence. With this view I have added the epithet real—meaning thereby an actual, veritable pirate, in contradistinction to your ideal Red Rovers, and all such kind of fanciful craft. My freebooter was alive and hearty but a few years since, and I presume he is so now, inasmuch as he was a middle-aged man, with a good constitution; and my story, if it has but a little romance in it, has a good deal of truth, which is something in these days of animal magnetism, spiritual knockings, and quack medicines.

But where shall I begin? Ah! I see—just off the Island of Flores, with Corvo, black as one of the crows from which it is named, far off in the distance to the north. Beautiful is the first land fall at sea, under any circumstances, and it may be imagined that it was with no ordinary feelings of pleasure that we gazed up the deep ravines and green valleys, dotted with occasional hamlets, churches and convents, and along the steep and rugged hill-sides of the northernmost of the Azores.

"Beautiful!" I exclaimed, as I stood upon the poop-deck of the corvette C***, with my spy-glass supported against the shrouds of the mizzen-rigging; "what a lovely and inviting valley!"

"Beautiful, indeed," replied one of the officers of the ship; "but did you ever hear that remark about distance lending enchantment to the view? If you were ashore there, you would find things of a different hue, I'll be bound. Those dark green slopes are nothing but potato patches, or what is equally unpicturesque, stumpy and bushy vineyards; and as for those pleasant-looking hamlets, I'll bet you couldn't get within fifty rods of them for the filth and stench with which they are surrounded. There is nothing like a Portuguese villa in the distance for an optical illusion."

The further discussion of the beauties of Flores, which, despite of the lieutenant's contemptuous opinion of Portuguese picturesqueness, seemed to be worthy of its name—the Island of Flowers—was interrupted by a midshipman, who, touching his cap to the officer of the deck, reported something floating in the water, a few hundred yards off the weather-beam.

"What does it look like?" demanded the lieutenant.

"Why, sir," replied the middy, "it looks to me like a bunch of sea-weed; but Jem Jones, of the fore-top, says he thinks it is something more than sea-weed; and Jones has got eyes like a hawk."

"Pshaw! it's nothing but some piece of a spar, with sea-weed collected round it. However, there is no harm in looking at it a little nearer. Take a pull on the larboard braces! luff up! luff up! Mr. P**** report to the captain a nondescript in sight to windward."

"Fore-top, there!" shouted the officer of the deck, in a few minutes after his order for bracing up the yards had been executed. "Fore-top, there! have you got your eyes open?"

"Aye, aye, sir."

"Well, what do you make out on the weather-bow?"

"A barrel or cask of some kind."

"A barrel! well, it's to be hoped there is something in it," observed the purser; "to-morrow is the Fourth of July: perhaps this is a god-send from old Neptune, in honor of the occasion."

The object was now plainly in sight, and the captain coming on deck, the ship was hove-to, and a boat lowered and sent for it. It proved to be what the topman had announced—a barrel; although, when close alongside, it was puzzle to me how any one could make out its character. Upon freeing it from sea-weed, and hoisting it on board, it was found to be completely enveloped in a mass of animal matter—barnacles, sea-suckers, long worms, and a kind of flat centipede, were intertwined in a firm and solid layer from three to four inches thick. The cooper was sent for, and after a good deal of active exertion, the head of the cask was exposed to view.

In the meantime there was much curious speculation afloat among the group of spectators, as to the time our prize had been in the water. Three years was the shortest period allotted by those who had had most experience of the sea; while among the junior officers there was a considerable diversity of opinion, and a much more liberal allowance of time to conjecture. "I'll tell you what I think," demurely interposed one of the younger middies—"you recollect that Columbus, when he was coming home on his first voyage, was caught in a terrible nor'wester just here, off the Western Islands, and in order that the knowledge of his great discovery might not be lost in case he foundered, as he was expecting to do every moment, he wrote two letters, enclosed them in tin cases with wax, put the cases in barrels, and then threw them overboard. There is no account of their ever having been picked up, and, of course, they must have been floating about till this time. I guess this is one of them."

"But the barrel is full of liquor of some kind," objected one of the bystanders.

"True," replied the middy; "but it is the sea-water that, in the course of three hundred and fifty years, has leaked in; we shall find the cake of wax inside all safe."

The carpenter having, at last, scraped his way down to the head of the barrel, proceeded to tap it with a gimlet. Upon canting the cask, a clear, colorless liquid streamed from the orifice, diffusing around a grateful fragrance, that made several old tars, who were assisting at the operation, snuff up the air with evident delight. A cup was brought and filled. The carpenter passing it to a midshipman, the midshipman to the first lieutenant, and the first lieutenant politely handing it on to the captain, who, nosing it with a dignified and pensive air for a moment or two, touched it to his lips, and handed it back to the first lieutenant.

The first luff raised it to his lips.

"Gin!" exclaimed the captain.

"Gin!" said the first luff.

"Very good!" said the captain.

"Devilish good!" responded the first luff.

At this moment the officer of the deck interposed to cut short the rising discussion. "That ship," said he, "to leeward, is acting in a queer kind of way. Since she was reported, about half an hour ago, she has altered her course, and is heading up for us as close as she can lie. She has signals flying, that I can make nothing of, at her fore and main-masts; but I can't tell whether she has a flag at her peak or not. I suppose she wishes to speak us."

"Well, sir, square away, and give her a chance to do so," replied the captain.

The attention of all the idlers was, by this order, directed to the advancing ship; and upon looking round again for the first object of interest—the barrel of gin—it had most mysteriously disappeared. There was a rumor current throughout the ship during the day, that the barrel had been seen on its way to the captain's store-room; but an extra glass of common ship's whiskey, given, ostensibly, in honor of the Fourth, but in reality, as Jack suggested, by way of commutation for his share of the prize, was all that was ever heard of that cask of well-seasoned Hollands.

The stranger having backed his main top-sail under our lee-quarter, announced, in answer to our hail—that he was an Englishman—a hundred and ten days from Sydney, in New South Wales, and that the day before he had been boarded by pirates.

At the bare mention of the word pirate, there was as strong a sensation throughout the ship—from knight-heads to taffrail—as ever ran through a New-York drawing-room upon the announcement of an English lord or a mustachoed French marquise. One of the quarter boats was at once lowered away, manned, and the first lieutenant placing himself in the stern-sheets, pushed off, and was soon on board the stranger. We had nothing to do but to await his return. In the meantime speculation was rife as to the circumstances of the piracy, and the probable whereabouts of the freebooters.

The report of the lieutenant, upon his return, was to the effect that the Englishman had been boarded early in the forenoon of the day before, by a boat from a clipper-built brig, after having been summoned to heave to by a shot from a long gun amidships. The brig showed no flag, but appeared to be well-manned with a Spanish-looking set of fellows, in red caps and blue woollen shirts; and in addition to the first gun, she carried three or four carronades on a side. Upon coming on board, the boat's crew at once set about plundering the ship, apparently seeking only such articles as they could use on the brig. In fact, the officer of the boat announced, in the politest manner, and in broken English, to the terrified passengers and crew, that his craft was merely short of sea-stores, and that he should simply help himself to such things as he stood in need of. How much of this forbearance was due to the fact that he knew there was hardly a possibility of there being any specie on board, and that the cargo was bulky, and of but little value, it is impossible to say. Having helped themselves to a new fore top-sail, several bales of canvass and rope, three or four barrels of pork and biscuit, and sundry articles from the tool-chest and steward's pantry, the pirates quietly got into their boats, and went off to their brig, which, without further notice, filled her main .top-sail, and stood off to the south-east.

A long passage had already greatly reduced the Englishman's stock of provisions, and the pirate's exactions left him with barely ten days' supply, even after putting all hands upon the shortest possible allowance. It was this that had made him so anxious to speak us. Supplying him with beef and bread enough to last him for the remainder of his voyage, we bade him good-bye, and hauling our wind, stood upon the track of the pirate.

Not a sail showed itself the rest of the day, although some two hundred pairs of eyes were kept on the stretch; and provoking enough it was, when to a dead certainty there was a pirate within a hundred miles of us. The next morning, however, we were gratified with the sight of a set of topgallant sails; but unfortunately then there were three of them, whilst the gentleman we were after carried but two, his vessel being a brig. It was thought, however, best to overhaul the ship in sight, and inquire if she had seen anything of the free-booter whose acquaintance we were so anxious to make. To do this it was necessary to haul up a little, as the ship was to windward; but to our surprise it was soon perceived that the stranger had followed our example, and braced up too. A still sharper pull on our lee braces produced a corresponding change in the stranger's course; and it was evident that, for some reason or other, he was indisposed to speak us. It would never do for a crack corvette to give it up so; and with everything set, alow and aloft, and bowlines hauled taut, we commenced a regular chase. At length we got near enough to send a shot dancing along on the water ahead of him, when he at once put his helm up and came down under our stern. She proved to be a beautiful Portuguese clipper-looking craft, with unmistakeable tokens of the slaver in every line of her finely-moulded hull, and in the spread of her square yards and taunt tapering topmasts. However, we had nothing to say to her or her business, and as she had seen nothing of the pirate, we filled away for Fayal, upon the suggestion of the first luff. "Who knows," says he, "but that the fellow has gone into Fayal—it is close by, and as he appears to have been short of grub, he has, perhaps, put in there for potatoes and onions. As to the onions, I'm sure he couldn't do better; for the Fayal onions are almost equal to those of Madeira, and the Madeira onions are famous the world over."

We came to anchor in the roadstead of Orta, amid a fleet of Yankee whale ships, who were laying in their stores of vegetables and fruits; but no pirate was to be seen.

Orta, with its whitewashed buildings, looks pleasant enough from the sea; but as soon as you set foot on shore you find yourself in a little filthy dilapidated town. The streets, perhaps, are not so disgustingly dirty as those of New-York; but they are very narrow, and the houses are old and mean. On the opposite side of the roadstead rises the beautiful Peak of Pico; its top covered with snow, and enveloped in fantastic and ever-varying clouds, and with its steep sides clothed with vineyards—from whence come the Pico wine of the New-York market, which is not unfrequently sold as Madeira.

There was no pirate; but as the first luff had promised us there were plenty of onions, "mild as new milk, and big as your hat," of which, with other fruits, we laid in a good store, inasmuch as it was whispered that we were going to run by Madeira without stopping at Funchal until our return.

Ten days from that time and we were becalmed, right under the famous Peak of Teneriffe. By this the excitement about the pirate had died away; the fellow had slipped off—not only out of the sight of the sharp eyes at our fore-topmast cross-trees, but apparently out of the minds of the loungers on the quarter-deck; and the conversation for the time flowed in two pretty nearly equal streams—one an abuse of the calm, and the other a laudation of the majestic Peak. *Pour passer le temps*, the deep sea lead was got overboard, but there was no bottom at hundreds and hundreds of fathoms. If the ocean ever dries up, so that the Peak of Teneriffe can be viewed from the present bottom of the surrounding sea, it will unquestionably be thought to be the most astonishing mountain in the world.

Every thing must have an end, even a calm in summer among the Canaries; and at last a gentle breeze and a favorable current set us around the island to the roadstead of Santa Cruz. There was quite a display of shipping at anchor, and the city looked really enchanting with its yellow and whitewashed buildings stretching along the foot of the craggy mountain. But it must be recollected that this was my first visit, and I had no idea of what a hot and disagreeable hole the chief town of Teneriffe really is.

"What a fine town," I exclaimed, as our gallant vessel was slowly creeping before the first light puffs of the sea-breeze into her anchorage.

"Fine town, indeed!" exclaimed the surgeon, who had had some experience of the place in a former visit; "a fine town for lazy priests, beggars, and fleas."

"That's true," interrupted the purser; "but I don't know that is any especial reproach to Santa Cruz. You may say it of almost any Spanish town that I have ever had the luck to visit."

And this is the land that was once peopled by the Guanchos; and it is the caverns of those precipitous rocks that are said still to hold their mummyfied remains. Mysterious people! who, it is said, reversing the usual order of things, allowed every woman two or more husbands. What an argument for Fourierism—not as bearing on the merits of that much talked of system, but as showing its possibility—as proving that in the social state there is nothing, however absurd or contrary to our reason or our prejudices, that may not, under certain circumstances, be done. And there are the very batteries, a shot from which, if I recollect aright, took off Nelson's arm one night, when he was out on boat service; and there, far away up the dark ravines stretch the vineyards that produce some of the finest wine in the world: albeit, the name Teneriffe has come to signify in the American market everything that is abominable in the vinous way.

My reflections were cut short by the rattle of the chain cable, as the anchor dropped from the bows. A boat was soon alongside with several dark-looking officials, in dingy gold lace, who proved to be health officers. *Pratique* was at once granted, and we had permission to communicate with the shore. In a man-of-war, coming from a healthy port, there is never much trouble with the quarantine; but in a merchant ship, nine cases out of ten, nothing can be more vexatious. Of all the modes of annoying a quiet voyageur, including custom-house regulations, passports, &c. there is nothing to equal the miserable, useless, and barbarous quarantine laws of about half the ports in the globe.

Our anchor was hardly down, and *pratique* obtained, when the captain's boat was ordered to be manned. It was decidedly uncommon and *infra dig.* for the skipper to hurry ashore in the first boat; and a good deal of conjecture was wasted as to what the old fellow had in his eye. The most reasonable supposition was, that he wanted to get the weather-guage of his middies with the black-eyed senoritas of Santa Cruz—a supposition that gained in strength when it was found that the first lieutenant had so much work for the men that no boat could go ashore for two or three hours. There was evidently collusion between the two oldest officers of the ship.

In about an hour's time a large boat, with two or three soldiers in the bow, and a couple of officers in the stern-sheets, came alongside. Upon being piped over with all honors, the elder of the two officers advanced to the first lieutenant, and presented to him a note. The lieutenant glanced his eye over it, and then politely led the way into the captain's cabin.

If conjecture was a little excited and wild before, it was now stark, staring mad. What could it all mean? And that last move of the first lieutenant—taking the Spaniards so suddenly into a secret consultation in the cabin!—that was a puzzler.

"Pshaw!" observed one; "that is only because he don't like to uncoil his Spanish here before us all, on the quarter-deck."

"Don't you believe that," replied another; "if there is anything the first lieutenant is proud of, it is his Spanish; and he'd uncoil it, fake after fake, on the quarter-deck of an admiral."

Conjecture was busy, as I have said, when the lieutenant opened the cabin door, and threw on fresh fuel by ordering a boat to be manned. As soon as it was ready he descended to the stern sheets. The Spanish officers took their places in their own boat, and both shoved off, but not in the direction of the landing.

We watched them as they wended their way among the shipping, until they brought up alongside a small, rakish-looking brig. Their arrival seemed to produce some excitement among her red-capped crew, who, we could see with our glasses, were at once mustered aft in presence of the lieutenant and the Spanish officials, while our boat's crew were observed to ascend the rigging, and casting off the gaskets, let the sails drop from the yards.

"The pirate!" exclaimed a half dozen of voices; and there she lay as plain as the day; there could be no doubt of it; the brig was unquestionably the freebooter of the Azores. All agreed that she had a wonderfully piratical air, but it was a little curious that it had taken the eye of our astute old skipper to first discover it.

And thus was explained the reason of his hurry to get ashore before anything could leak out, as to our knowledge, that a piracy had been committed. Upon landing he had at once an audience with the Governor General, and communicated to him his suspicion of the brig, which had come to anchor the evening before, and which had yet had no communication with the shore. The consequence was, an order to our first lieutenant to accompany the captain of the port on a visit to the suspected craft.

Upon loosing the sails, there hung the identical fore topsail, with all its marks, as described by the English captain; the bales of canvass and rope, with the names of the Sidney makers; and the barrels of beef and pork, with their English brands.

"But what will be done with him?" we demanded of the lieutenant, upon his return from the execution of his orders; "will they hang him?" "Hang him! not a bit of it; but they'll serve him almost as badly as if they did. He proves to be a rich fellow from the neighboring island of Grand Canary, who has for a long time been engaged in the slave trade. He has got money, and that will save his neck; but they'll strip him just as clean as they are now going to strip his brig;" and the lieutenant pointed to a score of red-capped sailors, who were busily engaged in unbending the brig's sails and sending down her spars.

The fleet clipper, that for years had eluded the English cruizers off the African coast, had at last fallen into the clutches of the half-starved officials of Santa Cruz. There could be no doubt of her fate; she would be condemned; while her captain, after being put through the squeezing processes of the Spanish courts, would be turned loose to commence again, if he could muster the capital, his trade of slaver and pirate.

"Pity we could not have overhauled him before he came to anchor," exclaimed the captain.

"And have sent him to the United States," replied the first lieutenant, "where he would have been at once discharged—an indignation meeting got up in his favor

—and ourselves served with writs for damages."

"Never!" replied the captain—"I would blow him out of the water sooner. No—I would have taken him into Gibraltar, and given him up to the authorities there. Gibraltar is not much of a town for sympathy; but then there is plenty of law and justice for such cases."

THE

ASTONISHING ADVENTURE

OF

JAMES BOTELLO.

To an author who has been accustomed to deal with the startling and the marvellous in the way of incident and adventure, nothing can be more amusing than the confident opinions of critics and readers as to the improbability, and frequently the impossibility, of particular scenes, which often happen to be faithful descriptions of actual occurrences. In this manner several passages from "Kaloolah" and "The Berber" have been indicated by some of my many good natured and liberal critics in this country and in England, as taxing a little too strongly the credulity of readers. Among such passages, the escape, in the first pages of the Berber, of the young Englishman, by jumping overboard in the bay of Cadiz, and hiding himself in the darkness of the night beneath the overhanging stern of his boat, has been particularly pointed out. Now, if this was pure invention, it might be safely left to a jury of Yankee boatmen or Spanish *barquéros* to decide whether the incident was not in the highest degree probable and natural; but being literally founded in fact, it is perhaps unnecessary to make any such appeal. There may be, however, a few unadventurous souls who will still persist in their doubts as to the probability of the incident. For the especial benefit of such I will relate the true story of a boat adventure, which in every way is a thousand times more strange and incredible than any of the wildest inventions of the wildest romance.

The voyage of Vasco di Gama around the Cape of Good Hope into the Indian Ocean was the beginning of a complete revolution in the trade of Europe and the East. This trade, which, following the expensive route of Egypt and the Red Sea, had been for a long time in the hands of the Venetians and Genoese, suddenly turned itself into the new and cheap channel opened by the enterprize of the Portuguese. The merchants of Genoa and Venice found themselves unexpectedly cut off from their accustomed sources of wealth, while a tide of affluence rolled into the mouth of the Tagus, and Lisbon became the commercial mart of the world.

The success of the Portuguese gave a new impulse to the spirit of enterprise which had already been excited among the maratime nations of Europe by the discoveries of Columbus, and efforts to divert a portion of the golden current soon began to be made. The Spaniards debarred from following the direct route of the Portuguese by their own exclusive pretensions in the west, and the consequent decision of the Pope, granting to them the sole right of exploration beyond a certain line of longitude to the west, and confining the Portuguese to the east, had, under the guidance of the adventurous Magellan, found a westerly route to the Indies. The English were busy with several schemes for a short cut to the northwest. The Dutch were beginning to give signs of a determination, despite the Pope's decision, to follow the route by the Cape of Good Hope. As may be imagined, these movements aroused the jealousy of the court and merchants of Lisbon. They trembled least their commercial monopoly should be encroached upon, and every care was taken to keep the rest of Europe in ignorance of the details of the trade, and of the discoveries and conquests of their agents in the East.

Of course nothing could be more injurious to a Portuguese of the time than to be suspected of a design to aid with advice or information the schemes of foreign rivals. Unluckily for James Botello such a suspicion lighted upon him. It was rumored that he was disposed to sell his services to the French. He was known to be a gentleman of parts, well acquainted with the East—having served with credit under the immediate successors of Vasco de Gama—and as competent as any one to lead the Frenchman into the Indian Ocean, and to initiate him into the mysteries of the trade. The suspicion, however, could not have been very strong, and probably had no real foundation in truth, or else more stringent measures than appears to have been used would have been adopted by an unscrupulous court to prevent his carrying his designs into execution. The rumor, however, had its effect; and Botello soon found that his influence at court was gone, and that he had become an object of jealous observation.

Anxious to give the lie to this calumny, and to regain the favor of his sovereign, John III, Botello embarked as a volunteer in the fleet which was taking out to Calicut, the new viceroy, De Cunna. Upon the arrival of this fleet, the operations of the Portuguese, both military and commercial, were carried on with renewed vigor; and in all these Botello bore his part, but without being able wholly to remove the suspicions with which he was sensible his actions were still watched by his superiors.

A favorite project of the Portuguese—one that had been pursued with energy and by every means of diplomacy or war—was the establishment of a fort in Diu, a town situated at the mouth of the Gulf of Cambaya. Several times the capture of the place had been attempted by force, but without success. Even the great Albuquerque had been foiled in a furious attack. Failing in this, the Portuguese repeatedly endeavored to get permission to erect a fort for the protection of their trade, by persuasion or artifice. It had become an object of the most ardent desire, as well with the king and court at home, as with the viceroys and their officers in the East.

It happened now in the year 1534, that Badur, king of Cambaya, was sorely pressed by his enemy the Great Mogul—so much so, that he was compelled to call in the assistance of his other enemy, the Portuguese. The price of this assistance was to be permission to erect and garrison a fort at Diu. Badur hesitated; he knew that if the Portuguese were allowed a fort, they would soon be masters of the whole town; but his necessities were urgent, and he finally acceded to the demand. De Cunna rushed to Diu; a treaty was speedily concluded with Badur—the fort was planned, and its erection commenced with vigor.

No one better than Botello knew how pleased King John would be with the news. He resolved to be the bearer of the good tidings, and thus to restore himself to the royal favor. His plan was a bold and daring one; in fact, considering the known dangers of the sea, and the then imperfect state of navigation, it must have seemed almost hopeless; but he suffered no doubts or apprehensions to prevent him from carrying it into immediate effect. In order to conceal his design, he gave out that he was going on a boat excursion up the Gulf of Cambaya, to visit the court of the now friendly Badur. Two young soldiers, of inferior degree, named Juan de Sousa and Alfonzo Belem, readily consented to accompany him. The boat selected for the voyage was a small affair—something like a modern jolly boat, though of rather greater beam in proportion to its other dimensions; its length was sixteen feet, its breadth nine feet. Four Moorish slaves from Melenda, on the coast of Africa, were selected to work the boat, while two native servants, having Portuguese blood in their veins, completed the crew.

Botello's preparations for the voyage were soon made; and waiting only to secure a copy of the treaty with Badur, and plans of the fort which had been commenced, he ordered the short mast, with its tapering lateen yard, to be raised, and the sail trimmed close to the breeze blowing into the roadstead of Diu. But instead of turning up along the northern coast of the Gulf of Cambaya, he directed the bow of his little bark boldly out to sea.

His companions knew but little of navigation; but they knew enough to know that a south-westerly course was hardly the one on which to reach Cambaya. To the remonstrances of Juan and Alfonzo, Botello simply replied that he preferred sailing south with the wind, to rowing north against it; and they would find the course he had chosen the safest and shortest in the end.

In this way they sailed for three days. On the morning of the fourth Botello found that it would be impossible for him longer to turn a deaf ear to the mutterings of discontent among his crew. It was high time for an explanation of his plans; and trusting to his eloquence and influence, he proceeded to unfold his design.

Imagine the astonishment and dismay depicted in the countenances of the servants and sailors when he told them that he purposed making the long and dangerous voyage to Lisbon in the miserable little boat in which they had embarked. But as he went on commenting upon the feasibility of the project, discussing the real dangers of such voyage, and ridiculing the imaginary, and dilating upon the honors and rewards which they would win by being the first bearers of the tidings they carried, a change from dismay to hope and confidence took place in the minds of all his hearers, excepting the African sailors, who did not much relish the idea of so long a voyage to Christian lands. They, however, were slaves and infidels, and their opposition was not much heeded.

To every objection Botello had a plausible reply. He confidently asserted his knowledge of a safe route, and of his ability to preserve their little craft amid all the dangers of the sea.

"But may we not be forstalled in our news, after all," demanded Alfonzo, "by the vessels from Calicut?"

"No fear of that," replied Botello. "The news from Diu will not reach Calicut for a month, and then it will be too late in the monsoon to despatch a vessel, even if one were ready. Besides, I have certain information that the viceroy has determined that no dispatches shall be sent home until he can announce the completion of the fort."

"I like not this new route you propose," said Juan. "Why leave the usual course to Melenda?"

"Because we should be in danger of exciting the suspicions of our brethren who now garrison the forts of Melenda, Zanzabar, and Mozambique, and perhaps be detained. No, we will take a more direct course—strike the coast of Africa below Sofalo, and then follow the shore around the Cape of Good Hope."

"And what are we to do for provisions and water, in the meantime?"

"Of provisions we have a store that will last until we reach land, when we can obtain supplies from the natives; as to water, we must go at once upon the shortest possible allowance, and daily pray for rain—St. Francis will aid us. I can show you something that will set your minds at ease upon that point."

Botello produced a box from beneath the stern sheets,

and opening it, took out with an air of reverence a leaden image of the saint.

"See this," he exclaimed, in a tone of exultation. "It was modelled from the portrait recognised by the aged Moor. Have you not heard of the miracle?—true, you were not at Calicut. Know, then, that a few months since, a native of India was presented to the viceroy, whose reputed age amounted to three hundred years. His story was, that in early youth he encountered an aged man lingering upon the banks of a stream which he was anxious to pass. The youth tendered the support of his strong shoulders, and bore him across the water. As a reward for the service, the old man bade the youth to live until they should meet again. And thus had he lived, until a few months since he was presented to De Cunna, when he at once recognised in a portrait of St. Francis the holy man whom he had carried across the stream. This image was modelled from that portrait; it was blessed by the pious convert in whose person was performed the miracle. Our voyage must be prosperous with this on board."

The sight of an image taken from a portrait acknowledged to be the saint himself, removed all doubt. And what Botello's arguments and persuasions might have failed to accomplish, was easily effected by the little image of lead. A heretic might, perhaps, have questioned the saint's power over the physical phenomena of the sea, but he could not have denied his moral influence over the minds of the adventurous voyagèurs who confided in him. No hesitation remained, except in the minds of the four slaves, who, having been forcibly converted from the errors of Mohammed, were yet somewhat weak in the true faith.

It was this want of faith that led to one of the most lamentable events of the voyage. They had been out more than a month without having had sight of land, and not even a distant sail had lighted up the dismal loneliness of the ocean. It must be recollected what a solitude was the vast surface of the Indian and Pacific seas in those days. Besides, the Portuguese fleets that followed each other at long and regular intervals, Christian commerce there was none, while Arabian trade was small in amount, and confined to certain narrow channels. The Moorish slaves had never before been so long in the open sea, and their fears increased as day after day the little boat bore them farther to the south. The provisions were also, by this time, nearly exhausted, and the daily allowance of water proved barely sufficient to moisten their parched lips. The slaves, after taking council among themselves, demanded that the course of the boat should be arrested.

"And which way would you go?" asked Botello. "Back to Diu? It would take three months to reach the port, and long ere that we should starve."

"Let us steer, then, directly for the African coast. Melenda must be our nearest port."

"Never!" returned the resolute Botello. "I will run no risk of having our voyage frustrated by the jealousy of my old enemy, Alfonzo Peristrello, who has command at that station. Courage for a few days more, and we shall see land. There are isles hereaway that you will deem fit residences for the blessed saints—such fruits! such flowers!"

The promises of Botello had influence with all of his companions excepting the Moors, whose muttered discontent suddenly assumed a fierce and menacing aspect. Luckily, Botello was as wary as he was brave.

It was in the middle of the night that, stretched upon the midship thwart of the boat, he noticed a movement among the Moors, who occupied the bow. One of them moved stealthily towards him, and bending over him, cautiously sought the hilt of his dagger; but before he could draw it, the grasp of Botello was upon his throat, and he was hurled to the bottom of the boat. With a shout, the other Moors seized the boat-hooks and stretchers, and rushed upon Botello; but Juan and Alfonzo were upon the alert, and, drawing their long daggers, rushed to his defence. Never was there a more desperate conflict than on that starlit night, in that frail boat, that floated a feeble, solitary speck of humanity on the bosom of the vast Indian sea.

The conflict was desperate, but it was soon over. The Portuguese of those days were other men than their degenerate descendants of the present age; and, besides, the slaves were overmatched both in arms and numbers. Three were slain outright, and the fourth driven overboard. One of the Portuguese servants was killed; thus diminishing the number of the voyagèurs more than one half—a lucky circumstance, without which, most probably, the whole would have perished.

For a week longer the little bark stood on its course, when a violent storm threatened a melancholy termination to the voyage. The wind, however, was accompanied by rain, and Botello kept up the spirits of his friends by attributing the storm to St. Francis, who had sent it expressly to save them from dying by thirst. It would have been perhaps more easy to believe in the saint's agency in the matter had there been less wind; for in addition to the danger of being engulfed by the heavy sea, their clothing, which they spread to collect the rain, was so deluged with salt spray as to make the water exceedingly brackish. Bad as it was, however, it served to maintain life until they reached a little rocky, uninhabited island in the channel of Mozambique.

It was with some difficulty that a landing place was found. Upon ascending the rocks, a few scattered palms exhibited the only appearance of vegetation.

Their chief necessity—fresh water—however, was found in abundance, standing in the hollows of the rocky surface, where it had been deposited by the recent storm. Several kinds of wild fowl showed themselves in abundance, and so tame as to suffer themselves to be caught without any trouble; while crowding the little sandy inlets were thousands of the finest turtle.

At this spot Botello and his companions rested for a week; which was spent in caulking and repairing their boat and sail, drying and salting the flesh of fowl and turtle, and in filling every available vessel with the precious fluid so liberally furnished by their patron, St. Francis.

A succession of storms followed their departure, and tossed them about here and there for so many days that their reckoning became exceedingly confused. Botello, however, was an accomplished navigator, and his sailor instinct stood him in good stead. Upon returning fair weather, he conjectured that he was abreast of Cape Corientes, and the bow of the boat was directed, due east, for the African coast.

Calms followed storms. The oars were got out, and day after day the clumsy boat was pulled through the long rolling swell of the glassy sea. Still no sight of land. Their provisions were getting short again—their water was reduced to the lowest possible allowance, and the labor of the oar was rapidly exhausting their strength. The image of St. Francis was hourly appealed to. Sometimes his aid was implored in most humble prayers—sometimes demanded with the wildest imprecations and threats. One day Botello seized the little St. Francis, and whirling him on high, threatened to throw him into the sea unless he instantly granted a sight of land; no land showed itself, and the saint was reverentially replaced in his box. But he was not to rest there long in quiet. The next day the ingenious Botello announced to his sinking companions that he had a plan to compel the saint to terms. The image was produced from its box, a cord was fastened around its neck, and it was then thrown overboard. Down went his leaden saintship into the depths of the ocean. "And there he shall remain," exclaimed Botello, "until he sends us land or rain." An hour had not expired when a faint bluish haze in the eastern horizon attracted all eyes. A favorable breeze springing up, the sail was hoisted, and as the boat moved under its influence the haze grew in consistency and size. Land was in sight.

The reader may perhaps smile with contempt at the superstitious faith of Botello and companions in the connexion between this happy land-fall and their ingenious compulsion of the saint's miraculous power; but it may be questioned whether there was not good ground for their belief—at least as good ground as there is for faith in any of the facts of animal magnetism, clairvoyance, and spiritual rappings.

The land proved to be a point in Lagca Bay—a familiar object to Botello. Upon going ashore, a party of natives received him, with whom friendly relations were soon established, and from whom provisions and water were readily obtained. A few days served to recruit the exhausted strength of the party, when taking again to their boat, they coasted along the shore, landing at frequent intervals, until they reached the dreaded Cape of Storms, as the southern point of Africa was called by its first discoverer, Bartholemew Diaz.

The Cape did not belie its reputation. From the summit of Table Mountain, and the surrounding high lands, it sent down a gust that drove the unfortunate voyagéurs away from the land a long distance to the southwest; and many weary and despairing days were past before they were able to make the harbor of Saldahana. Here the chief necessity of life—fresh water—was found in abundance, and a supply of provisions obtained, consisting chiefly of the dried flesh of seals, with which the harbor was filled. A few orange and lemon trees, planted by the early Portuguese discoverers, were loaded with fruit, and afforded a grateful and effectual means of removing the symptoms of scurvy which were beginning to appear.

Saldahana being a resting place for the outward

bound Portuguese fleets, Botello made his stay as short as possible, lest he should be intercepted and turned back by some newly appointed and jealous viceroy. For the same reason he avoided several points on the coast of western Africa where his countrymen had stations—keeping well out to sea and from the mouth of the Congo, and steering a direct course across the Gulf of Guinea. He knew that if a Portuguese admiral had sailed at the appointed time, he must be somewhere in that Gulf, and that his tall barks would hug the shore, creeping from headland to headland slowly and cautiously. The energetic Botello and his companions had encountered too many dangers to be frightened at the perils of a run across the Gulf, and the resolution was adopted to give the Portuguese fleet, by the aid of St. Francis, the go-by in the open sea.

The run was successfully achieved; not, however, without many weary days at the oar, and many an appeal to St. Francis for favoring winds, and for aid in the sudden tornados which frequently threatened to engulf them. Cape de Verd was reached; the barren shore of the great desert was passed, with but a single stoppage in the Rio del Ouro—a slender arm of the sea setting up a few miles into the sands of Sahara. Here a few dates and some barley cakes were purchased of a family of wandering Arabs; and again putting to sea, the shores of Morocco were cautiously coasted. Without further adventure, but not without further suffering, and labor, and danger, the short remaining distance was passed. The head of the Straits of Gibraltar—the headlands of Spain—the southern point of Algarve, successively came in sight; and then the smiling mouth of the golden Tagus greeted their longing eyes.

And thus was happily finished this wonderful voyage—a voyage which, if performed in the present day, with all the means and appliances of navigation, would excite the admiration of the world, but which, under the circumstances of the age, the prejudices and ignorance of the voyagéurs, and the imperfect state of maritime science, may truly be considered the most astonishing upon record. It must be observed, too, that this was no involuntary boat expedition—no desperate alternative of some foundering ship's crew—but the deliberate, carefully considered project of an experienced sailor; and that the hardihood evinced in its conception was surpassed by the resolution, perseverance, and skill with which it was conducted to its end.

The presence of Botello was soon known to his friends; and the rumor spread through the city that an Indian fleet had arrived off the mouth of the Tagus. It reached the court, so that upon his application for an audience of the king, he found no detention except from the curiosity of the courtiers and ministers; which, however, he resolutely refused to satisfy, until he had communicated his news to the royal ear.

Botello exhibited his copy of the convention with Badur, king of Cambaya, and the plans of the fort which was being erected at Diu, and related the history of his adventurous voyage. King John freely expressed his astonishment and delight, and calling around him the members of his household, familiarly questioned Botello as to all the little details of his voyage.

There was a pause in the conversation. Botello threw himself upon his knees. "There is one point," he exclaimed, "upon which your majesty has not condescended to question me."

"What is that?" demanded the king.

"My reasons," replied Botello, "for undertaking this long and hazardous voyage. Your majesty knows, or at least many of your majesty's enemies know, that I am one not over cautious in confronting danger, either by sea or land; but I should never have had the courage to make myself the bearer of tidings however important, as I have done, without some reason other than the desire of astonishing the world by a feat which by many will be pronounced simply fool-hardy. Your majesty will believe me—I had another and a better reason."

"And that reason was——"

"The favor of my sovereign, and the removal of

the undeserved suspicions with which my motives and feelings had been visited."

"Rise," replied the king, extending his hand, and smiling graciously. "Our suspicions were of the slightest. We will take some fitting opportunity of showing that they are gone for ever."

The courtiers overwhelmed Botello and his companions with congratulations. The king accompanied him to see the boat, and upon dismissing him, renewed his assurances of favor and reward—assurances which Botello found were destined never to be realized. The next day a change had come over the royal countenance—the jealousy of trade had been aroused. It would be a terrible blow to the commercial monopoly, already threatened from so many quarters, to have it known that the voyage from the East Indies had been performed in an open boat. Botello was informed that, for reasons of state, his boat must be destroyed, but that he himself should ever continue to enjoy the favorable opinion of his sovereign. As an earnest of the royal favor, which was some day to exhibit itself more openly, he was appointed to an office of no great consequence, and which had also the disadvantage attached to it of a residence in the interior of the country.

Once installed, he found that he was little better than a prisoner for life. His movements were closely watched by the officials surrounding him; his communications with the capital were cut off, and to all his remonstrances and petitions the only reply was that the king's service required his continual residence in his department. Botello was not a man to quietly submit to such unjust restraint; but unluckily his health began to fail. His body found itself unable to withstand the chafings and struggles of his energetic and adventurous spirit under the mortifications and disappointments of his position; and the fears and suspicions of the court of Lisbon were soon removed by his death. His boat had been burned—his companions had been sent back to India, and it was not long before the fact of his extraordinary voyage had passed from the public mind.

A good pendant to this story of Botello's adventure is the singular voyage made not many years since by a gallant and well known officer of the American navy. He still lives in the enjoyment of the highest honors of the service—the merited rewards of a life of extraordinary adventure and vicissitude.

Commencing life as a cabin-boy in the merchant service, his first voyage was to the West Indies. Upon his return his whole wages, amounting to one dollar, were judiciously expended for vaccination. Having thus secured an immunity from one of the worst forms of disease, and one to which sailors are peculiarly exposed, he again shipped, and for several years remained roving the ocean, under almost every conceivable circumstance, and in almost every possible position. He was wrecked several times, captured by a French privateer in our *quasi* war with France, confined some time in a Spanish prison at Santa Cruz, in the Canaries, and engaged in many stirring adventures; until, finally, as sailing master of an American corvette, he signalized his coolness and thorough seamanship by handling her, during a most desperate engagement with an English vessel, as if, to use the expression of his commanding officer, "he had been working her into some familiar roadstead."

It was in the earlier part of his career that the very singular voyage to which we allude took place. It happened that in the course of his rovings he found himself at Princes Island, in the Gulf of Guinea, the master of a small boat of not more than thirty tons. Here he was confined for several weeks by an attack of the coast fever. As soon as he was able to walk, he mustered his crew, which consisted of one old man and a boy—boarded his little craft, and got under way. The old man was also just recovering from the fever, and on the second or third day out, had a relapse, which laid him in his berth in the little confined cabin delirious. In a day or two more the captain himself was taken down again—the fever redeveloping itself in full force. No one now remained on deck of the little craft but the boy ; who was, however, under the circumstance, quite competent to the whole duty. The trade wind blew steadily. Pernambuco, their destined port, lay almost dead to leeward; and the little vessel, with her helm lashed and her foresail squared, steered herself on her westerly course without much trouble.

And fortunate it was that the wind was so steady, and that the boat could steer herself; for she was destined to be relieved of even the superintendence of the boy. There was a heavy sea on, before which she was industriously working her way—rolling, and pitching, and scudding but ever keeping herself buoyant and dry—when one day, as the boy was going aft with something that he had prepared for the invalids below, a short, sharp lurch threw him from his balance; a low rail, not more than a foot in height, but ill supplied the place of bulwarks, and over this the poor fellow tumbled into the sea. His wild shrieks pierced the ears of the sick men below, but could not arrest the course of the now masterless boat.

From this time for a period of two weeks, neither of the invalids were able to put a head above the deck. Still the boat bowled along in safety, at the rate of eight or ten knots an hour, before the stiff breeze. What a picture! could one have seen her struggling like a thing of life and volition—a little phantom or fairy bark—with the rough seas: now tossed aloft on their feathered crests, now sliding along their glassy sides, and now buried in their deep hollows—with no mortal hand to guide her—no indication of humanity about her rigging or on her deck—not even a sign of the freight of human misery she carried.

At the end of this period the captain, who, like his companion, had passed the greater part of the time in a state of stupor, interrupted only now and then by an instinctive application to the can of fresh water, luckily standing within reach, recovered his consciousness, and with it sufficient strength to creep from his berth, and to draw himself up the narrow companion-way. It was early in the morning: the sun was just beginning to pour his enlivening rays over the eastern ocean; the cool fresh breeze was stealing along the surface of the water, with healing on its wings, invigorating sensibly with every breath the invalid, and enabling him to reply to a hail from a lofty ship close along side of him, and standing on the same course.

"Where from, and where are you bound to?" demanded the stranger.

"From the coast of Africa, and bound to Pernambuco," replied the sick man. "But we have all been down with the African fever. There has not been a soul upon deck for many days, or weeks, for aught I know; and we have lost our reckoning entirely. Can you tell me what quarter of the world this may happen to be?"

"You look as if you had a hard time of it," returned the stranger; "but I don't see how you can say you have kept no reckoning. Your craft steers herself: there is nothing strange in that, going before the wind with nothing but head sail set; but she must have something of the pointer breed to nose her true course out for weeks. You are bound for Pernambuco, you say? Well, here is Pernambuco; you have hit it exactly. When this haze lifts you will see the landmarks."

And thus was happily terminated a voyage, the like of which never before occurred, and never, probably, will occur again. To cross the Atlantic, and that, too, not at its narrowest part, without any one to manage the vessel for more than two-thirds of the distance, is, considering the endless variety of accidents at sea, within perhaps the category of probabilities; but to hit exactly the port for which the voyage was originally commenced, we can hardly expect to happen a second time.

DRAGUT, THE CORSAIR.

CHAPTER I.

THE reader will recollect the Spanish ballad with the above title, in Lockhart's collection. It purports to illustrate an incident in the life of Rais Dragut, the most redoubted corsair, not even excepting the Barbarossas, who ever ranged the Mediterranean. But it must be observed that the Spaniard was Dragut's deadly enemy; and that in searching for materials for a sketch of his life, the poet is the only authority we have been able to find for the story told in the following lines:

" Oh swiftly, very swiftly, they up the straits have gone !
" Oh swiftly flies the corsair, and swift the cross comes on !
" The cross upon yon banner, that streams unto the breeze :
" It is the sign of victory—the cross of the Maltese.

" 'Row, row, my slaves,' quoth Dragut, 'the knights, the knights are near !
" Row, row, my slaves, row swiftly, the starlight is too clear ;
" The stars they are too bright, and he that means well,
" He harms us when he trims his light—yon Moorish sentinel.'

"Here came a wreathe of smoke from out a culverine—
"The corsair's stern it broke, and he sank into the brine;
"Down Moor and fettered Christian went beneath the billow's roar;
"But hell had work for Dragut, and he swam safe ashore.

The ballad goes on to relate how

"One only of the captives, a happy man is he:
"The Christian sailors see him yet struggling in the sea;
"They hear the captive praying—they hear the Christian tongue,
"And swiftly from the galley a saving rope is flung."

But it is not alone in the songs of his enemies that the famous Dragut established his renown. Among the Moors of Barbary his memory is still cherished, and his praises chaunted in verse. An aged Jew, a native of Fez, once assured us that in his youth many songs and stories of which Dragut's courage and prowess formed the staple, were current. He could recollect only the commencement of one, which ran nearly in this wise, making a somewhat curious counterpart to the Spanish song:

Ho! see the Knights of Malta—their coward cheeks are pale;
And, hark! from Spain and Italy there comes a fearful wail;
For Dragut, the bold corsair, has left Mahedea's shore,
And soon the trembling Christians shall hear his cannon's roar.

Haste! haste thee, Rais Dragut! up, Lion of the Sea!
Before thy flaunting banner the trailing cross doth flee;
Ho! charge the forward culverine! Ha! listen to the roar!
And, see! a mast is splintered! disabled is an oar!

The Christian hounds are quailing—'tis vain to fight or fly:
"Who may withstand bold Dragut!" is now their doleful cry;
While their Moorish slaves uprising wave aloft their joyful hands,
And clank to the name of Dragut their heavy iron bands.

Unlike the Barbarossas, and many other famous corsairs, who were renegados from the Christian faith, Dragut had the advantage of having been born a Mohammedan. His parents were poor laboring people, of a small village of Anatolia, lying opposite to the island of Rhodes. When a boy he was noticed for his adventurous and energetic spirit, and for an indisposition for the laborious and regular mode of life of his parents, who obtained a miserable living by tilling the soil. At twelve years of age young Dragut's budding genius had already outgrown the narrow boundaries of his native village; so, leaving home—whether with or without the paternal blessing, the historians do not say—he entered into the service of a master gunner in one of the galleys of the grand signior's fleet. His activity and intelligence soon procured him promotion; first from cabin-boy to sailor, then to pilot, and finally to gunner, in the duties of which latter station he became wonderfully expert. By the time that he had grown to manhood he had seen a great deal of active service, and had acquired no little reputation for courage and skill in navigation, but above all for the possession of resources in difficult straits.

Having saved a small sum of money, he purchased a share in an armed galley, in which he made several successful cruizes along the coasts of Italy. His portion of the plunder soon enabled him to possess a galley of his own. As he had no slaves to man the oars, he persuaded his crew to take upon themselves that labor, and to put to sea, trusting to fortune to supply the deficiency. Nothing could indicate a greater degree of confidence in his judgment and skill on the part of his followers. A well-timed descent upon a little fishing village on the coast of Sicily justified their faith in his good fortune, and a corps of stout, practiced rowers completed the galley's sailing trim.

The genius of Dragut had, heretofore, been cramped and confined; it had now an opportunity to display itself. With unflagging energy he traversed the Mediterranean from the mouths of the Nile to the Straits of Gibraltar, overhauling and capturing every merchant vessel he encountered, evading with singular address the armed galleys of the Knights of Malta, looking into every bay and inlet on the Christian coasts, and making many devastating inroads far into the country.

As his fame spread, other corsairs became desirous of uniting their fortunes with his; and ere long he found himself in command of quite a formidable squadron. At this time Heyreden Barbarossa, who had succeeded his brother in the government of Algiers, was the nominal chief of all Turkish corsairs in the Mediterranean, although it was not until sometime later that he received the appointment of Captain Basha, or commander-in-chief of all the Ottoman fleets. The ambition of Dragut expanding with his growing wealth and power, made him desirous of the official sanction of the Turkish government, and of the countenance and protection of Heyreden. Accordingly, proceeding to Algiers, he made an offer of his services, and an acknowledgment of the authority of the Basha, and of his master the Grand Signior. The reputation of Dragut had preceded him, and his reception by Barbarossa was of the warmest kind. His experience—his prudence and courage—and, above all, his intimate knowledge of every port in the Mediterranean, rendered him a valuable acquisition, and insured his appointment to the most important posts. He was intrusted with the conduct of several difficult and dangerous expeditions, in all of which he was successful; and was finally, after several years' service, nominated by the Basha his *Kayia*, or lieutenant, and given the sole command of a fleet of heavy galleys. Uncontrolled now, except by the promptings of his own energetic spirit, Dragut passed most of his time at sea. The coasts of Spain and Italy suffered terribly from his visitations; thousands of Christians were hurried into captivity, and the commerce of the Mediterranean was nearly annihilated.

It must not be supposed, however, that Dragut's successes secured any immunity to Mohammedan commerce. The Christian corsairs were numerous and active: retaliatory visits were paid to the coasts of Barbary and the ports of the Levant; and not an act of violence or cruelty was performed on one side, without its being paralleled, if not justified, by a similar deed on the other.

Among these Christian corsairs, the most formidable to the Barbary and Turkish cruizers were the renowned Knights of St. John. For awhile after their expulsion from their stronghold in the island of Rhodes, by Suleiman the Magnificent, the order declined in power; but its services were too valuable as a defence against the infidel for it to be suffered to go entirely to decay, and Charles the Fifth of Spain, the most powerful and politic prince of the time, presented to the wandering and homeless Knights the Island of Malta, a position admirably adapted to their chief object, that of war with the Infidel, and the protection of Christian commerce. From this central and commanding stronghold the order sent forth its cruizers, to slay, capture, and plunder with as little mercy as characterized the depredations of Dragut, Drubdevil, or the Barbarossas. Sad was the fate of the Christians who fell into the hands of the fanatical soldiers of the crescent; but equally sad was the fate of the captives of the stern and bigotted defenders of the cross.

The Abbe Vertot relates an incident which, although occurring in the case of a Mohammedan captain, illustrates equally well the feeling entertained by the Moorish galley slaves for their masters. The commander De Romegas was the most intrepid and successful knight that ever threw the banner of his order to the breeze. But he had a peculiarly ferocious aspect, and the reputation of treating his prisoners with great cruelty. He himself, however, asserted that he did so only by way of reprisal, and in order to force the Moorish corsairs to treat their Christian slaves with more humanity. This apology, however, says Vertot, did not entirely remove the suspicion entertained by the world that he, in resorting to retaliation, had not committed any great violence upon his nature; and that his temper, which was naturally cruel and violent, had perhaps contributed as much to it as policy. Certain it is, had the positions of himself and Rais Conciny been reversed, he would have suffered from the hands of his Moorish rowers the same fate that befell that famous corsair at the hands of his Christian slaves. It was a desperate battle that, between Romegas and Conciny. The galley of the Calabrian renegado was strongly manned—having two hundred and fifty Moorish soldiers, and two hundred Christians chained to the oar. For a long time the fight was maintained with equal advantage. When at last Romegas, enraged at such a vigorous resistance, collected his bravest officers, and leaped aboard the enemy, sword in hand. The corsair received him with similar resolution—killing two knights with his own hand; but staggering from a blow, he fell upon the rowers' benches, when the slaves seized him, and passed him along from bench to bench. "Every one gave him a blow, and some were so furious with revenge, that they tore him with their teeth. There was not one but would have a piece of him; so that before he was got to the last bench there was scarce a bit of him left."

CHAPTER II.

It was one bright morning in the summer of 1540 that a fleet of thirteen galleys were seen lying at anchor in the road of Geralatta, on the coast of Corsica, between Calvi and Liazzo. The garrison of the little castle on the shore, although secure from an assault, were terribly frightened; for they recognised in the flags flying at bow and stern the signals of the dreaded Dragut. Several of the galleys were lying within reach of the guns of the castle; but it was judged most prudent not to awaken the ire of the pirate, and provoke him to land, by opening a fire upon them.

Dragut himself well knew the prudential reasons restraining the garrison of the castle, and felt himself perfectly secure. It was not the first time that he had used the same roadstead for the purpose of resting his rowers, and waiting for his prey. As the sun rose, he emerged from his narrow cabin. A slave brought out a small praying rug of Turkish manufacture, and spread it upon the deck. Before seating himself upon it, Dragut threw from beneath his thick overhanging brows a keen glance, full of the instinctive comprehensiveness of the practised seaman, along the decks of his own galley, and over the other vessels of his squadron. The Moorish sailors and soldiers were busy; some cleaning their arms—others mending the rigging—others cooking their morning meal over little portable charcoal furnaces. The Christians were, some of them, still sleeping on their benches, to which they were chained; while others of them, awakened to their misery, were eating, with sighs, and half suppressed groans and muttered imprecations, their rations of black mouldy bread, dipped in a little rancid oil. A more woe-begone set can hardly be imagined. Begrimmed with dust, covered with sores, ragged and emaciated, there was the grim, stern-visaged Spaniard; the fierce-eyed, sharp-featured Italian; and scattered here and there, the white-haired German, and the stout-limbed Englishman—France alone furnishing no specimen of her people; her king, Henry II, happening to be at this time in alliance with the Porte. Little did these poor wretches dream of the sudden and happy turn of fortune that one short hour would produce.

Dragut scanned the horizon seaward for a moment. There was not a sail in sight; and the pious rover dropping upon his carpet, with his face to the east, addressed himself to his devotions. His prayers, however, were cut short by a sudden sensation throughout the deck, and the announcement that two galleys were sweeping around a point of land forming the mouth of the harbor. Dragut sprang to his feet, and rapidly issued his orders to slip the cables and give chase. The sleeping and listless slaves were aroused by blows, kicks, and curses, and the oars got into the water; but before any of the galleys could get in motion, another heavy vessel appeared in sight—and still another, and another; and instead of attempting to fly, upon the sight of the Moorish squadron, they proceeded to close up, and continued to advance into the harbor. Other galleys followed, until the astonished Algerines saw themselves shut in by a force three times as great as their own.

This force proved to be a fleet despatched expressly by order of Charles the Fifth, to capture the renowned corsair, or drive him from the Italian and Spanish coasts. Wearied out with the frequent complaints made to him of Dragut's depredations, the emperor had at last ordered Prince Andrea D'Oria, his admiral, to "hunt him out, and endeavor by all possible means to purge the seas of so insufferable a nuisance." The aged admiral received the order with pleasure, and hastened to fit out with the utmost secrecy and expedition a formidable fleet. Satisfied, however, with the glory he had already won, and anxious to advance the interests of his nephew, the prince transferred the command of the expedition to young Jannetin D'Oria, who, setting sail, had the good fortune to alight, without loss of time, upon the object of his search in the harbor of Giralatta.

The surprise was complete. Dragut saw that there was hardly a single chance of escape; but great as was the disparity of force, he got his galleys under way, and resolutely advanced to the attack. The battle raged with great violence for some time; but vain were all his efforts to force his way through the Spanish fleet. Gradually closing in, the heavy Christian vessels drove his galleys back towards the bottom of the bay, and within reach of the guns of the castle. The garrison opened upon him a furious fire; while the noise of the cannonade brought down to the shore a multitude of armed Corsican peasants, ready to attack him in case he should attempt to land.

Dragut seeing that the day was lost, consented to hoist a white flag in token of submission. A boat was despatched to the Spanish admiral, offering to capitulate upon terms; but D'Oria knew too well his advantages. The only condition he would grant was that of life; and with this Dragut was compelled to comply. The Algerine galleys were boarded by prize crews, the Christian slaves liberated, and the Mohammedan sailors and soldiers chained to the oars in their place.

Dragut was taken to the admiral's galley. He mounted to her deck with a dignified air, expecting to see in his captor the venerable and renowned Prince D'Oria. What was his surprise when he was presented to the youthful Jannetin. His pride was touched; rage flashed from his eyes, and in a voice trembling with passion he exclaimed: "What! have I then become the slave of such an effeminate, beardless boy!" Other hasty and passionate expressions escaped him, and among them a term of reproach which we cannot repeat, but which still occupies a prominent place in the slang vocabularies of the Mediterranean.

"Dog of an Infidel!" shouted the young prince. And rushing upon the sturdy and undaunted corsair, he struck him in the face, pulled off his turban, tore out his beard and mustachos, and would have run him through with his sword, had he not been restrained by his officers.

This singular scene exerted a most injurious influence upon the fortunes of Dragut. At the command of the enraged D'Oria he was loaded with fetters and chained to an oar. His propositions for ransom were treated with contempt, and he was given to understand that no considerations, not even all the wealth of Algiers, would move the admiral to his release.

The capture of the redoubted rover excited the strongest sensation throughout all the ports of the Mediterranean. Bonfires, illuminations, and processions attested the joy of the Christians; while the prompt efforts of the Algerine and Turkish governments to effect his liberation, testified to their sense of the loss the Moorish flag had sustained. Heyraden Barbarossa sent to offer in exchange any number of Christian slaves, or any sum his captors should choose to name, as a ransom. But vain were all the exertions of his friends; and the hard lot of the galley slave—to be daily reviled, beaten, starved, and finally worked to death at the oar—seemed to be the fate from which there was no possibility of escape.

CHAPTER III.

YEARS passed, when one day the Genoese were startled by the appearance of a hundred Turkish ships of war before their harbor. It was the fleet of Heyraden Barbarossa, who had been removed from the post of Basha of Algiers, and appointed by Suleiman to the office of Captain Basha, or commander-in-chief of all the naval forces of the Porte. The Genoese were taken quite by surprise. They had no force at hand adequate to the protection of their coasts from the attacks of such a powerful fleet, and of course were terribly alarmed, and ready to listen to whatever terms the Turkish admiral had to propose.

Barbarossa simply demanded that Dragut should be given up to him, promising that, in case his demand should be complied with, he would leave the coasts and commerce of the republic untouched, and that he would pay the sum of three thousand ducats for his ransom; and threatening, in case of refusal, to ravage with unheard of severity every accessible district. The Genoese were well satisfied to get rid of Barbarossa's presence so easily. The senate hastened to solicit from Admiral D'Oria the release of Dragut. His chains were knocked off; and the wretched galley-slave, who for four tedious years had tugged in sullen resignation at the oar, was once more a free man. Dragut was received on board the Turkish Admiral with every demonstration of respect; his friend and patron presenting him with a stout galliot, and a commission from the grand signior constituting him generalissimo of all the western corsairs.

An evil day for the Christians was that on which Dragut was restored to freedom. The cruelty with which, for four long years, he had been treated, had by no means improved his temper, or lessened his hatred of the followers of the cross. His old profession was resumed, and prosecuted with renewed ardor. In command of a powerful squadron, he daily made descents upon the coasts of his enemies, and committed the most terrible devastations. The Bay of Naples was visited by him in 1548. Castle Lamare was attacked and plundered, with various other towns and villages, and a multitude of people of both sexes, and all ages and conditions, carried off captive. A few days after a Maltese galley fell into his hands, on board of which he found seventy thousand ducats, designed for the repairs of the fortifications of Tripoli—an irreparable loss to the town, and a severe blow to his most inveterate enemies, the Knights of Malta.

This same year died the venerable and renowned Heyraden Barbarossa, at the advanced age of eighty. To repair the loss of his great admiral the grand signior issued an order that all Turkish and Barbary corsairs should render obedience of Dragut, as their captain-general; but while thus bestowing the authority, the title of captain-basha, through some court jealousy, was withheld. Dragut, however, was not a man to trouble himself about so small a matter as the title of an office. Substantial and available power was the object of his ambition, and to obtain this he resolved to imitate the example of Barbarossa the First, and secure a stronghold for himself on the southern shore of the Mediterranean, which he could make a depot for prizes, and a safe naval station for his own and the galleys of his dependants, and where, under the nominal protection of the grand signior, he could erect an independent principality.

Entertaining this design, he collected a squadron; and in mid-winter, when the Christian fleets had abandoned the sea, he attacked and made himself master of the Monester, Susa, and Fugues—three small towns belonging to the kingdom of Tunis, but which, from their defenceless position, had frequently changed masters, and were then in possession of the Spaniards. Dragut satisfied himself that neither of these places could be made tenable against the imperial fleet which would visit them in the spring. A stronger and more defensible position was necessary for his purposes—and he cast his longing eyes upon the fine city of Mahedia: but how to get possession of it was a question that any one but Dragut would have despaired of answering.

This city, supposed to be the Adrumetum of the Romans,* had, after undergoing many vicissitudes, fallen into utter decay, when Mahedi, the first Caliph of Kayrwan, rebuilt it, and gave it his own name. It occupied a peninsula running into the sea, which, where it joined the land, was not more than two hundred and fifty paces across. Its natural position, surrounded on three sides by water, and the extensive fortifications erected by Mahedi, rendered it one of the strongest places in Barbary. Substantial walls of solid masonry, flanked by six great towers, encompassed it. These walls were so thick that six horsemen could ride abreast upon them. Four of the towers were square,

* Dr. Shaw is of a different opinion. He thinks Herkla, a town situated twenty-five or thirty miles further to the northwest, to have been the Adrumetum of the Ancients, and that Mahedia is the *Turres*, or country seat of Hannibal, from which he is said to have embarked after his flight from Carthage.

of solid rock as high as the plinth, like the wall, and projected outwardly forty feet, as far as the barbacan of the ravelin. The towers next the sea were round, and constructed with an equal regard to strength. Each of these towers constituted a separate fortress, and could be entered only by little doors—so low that no one could pass without stooping. Besides these large towers there were numerous smaller ones, and outworks. On the land side there stood a large castle, built within double walls, between which was a space occupied by the soldiers' barracks. The only entrance to the city on the land side seems to have been through a gate and arched passage running under the large square tower on the eastern angle.

This kind of entrance is a peculiar and striking feature of Saracenic fortification. It consisted in this case of an irregular vaulted arch, seventy feet in length. Six double doors, covered with iron plates, defended the gloomy and imposing passage. The last door, towards the town, was composed wholly of heavy iron bars, crossed and recrossed, and firmly rivetted together. The form of the doors was slightly convex outwardly. They were furnished with portcullisses sliding in grooves from the top of the tower, and were ornamented with bronze lions in relief.

Lying within the walls there was a basin three hundred feet square, intended for galleys and small vessels; while for those of larger size there was a convenient harbor, protected by the defences of the town.

The environs corresponded in beauty and fertility to the wealth and strength of the place. Fronting the city on the south ran a ridge of rising hills, covered with vineyards and bespangled with gleaming pleasure houses; and on the east stretched a fine reach of ever-verdant gardens and orchards. Behind these was a ridge hills, of and beyond these again some spacious plains, abounding with excellent pasture, to which the Arabs were accustomed to resort in the winter with their vast herds of cattle.

In short, Mahedia was just the city to excite the longing of a rover in want of a permanent location—it was just the city in which to shed the coarse tarry garments of the common corsair, and assume the purple and fine linen of a sovereign prince. Dragut resolved to make himself master of it.

At this time Mahedia, having thrown off its allegiance to the kings of Tunis, was an independent city, and governed by a council of its chief inhabitants. These, although Mohammedans, were as little disposed to submit to Turkish rule as to Christian; and the movements of the corsairs were watched with great jealousy. There was nothing, however, to excite alarm; when one day a small Turkish brigantine sought an entrance into the harbor. Permission was readily accorded, especially when it was known that the famous Dragut, with whom the citizens were disposed to cultivate friendly terms, was on board.

Several times did Dragut visit the place: each time with only a single vessel, and always conducting himself with so much courteousness and affability, that the citizens were quite charmed with him. Accidentally, as it were, Dragut formed an acquaintance with Ibrahim Barat, one of the principal citizens, and commander of one of the towers. This acquaintance gradually ripened into intimacy, as many curious and costly presents found their way into the Moor's possession. At length Dragut held out the prospect of a partnership in the corsair business, and dazzled his eyes with visions of the immense profits which would surely result.

"But," continued Dragut, "to make a partnership safe and durable, it will be necessary to admit me to the privileges of a citizen. The proposition is more for your interest than mine."

The countenance of Barat fell as he thought of the cautious jealousy of his compatriots; but his cupidity, so artfully excited by the wily rover, would not permit him to hesitate, and he promised to make the attempt to secure for the corsair the freedom of the city.

Barat made his proposition to the council. Despite, however, his personal influence, it was rejected unanimously, and a vote of censure was passed upon him for proposing any connection with a corsair—a connection which, if once formed, would bring before the city the imperial fleet of Spain and Naples, and perhaps embroil them with the Turks. Barat was terribly enraged at the result of his application to the council. His vanity was mortified by the reprimand he had received; and Dragut found him in a mood that disposed him to listen to any propositions.

Everything was arranged between them. In pursuance of the plan agreed upon, Dragut withdrew from the city; and in order to wipe off the remembrance of his design, and disperse the jealousy which the magistrates might entertain on that account, several weeks were suffered to elapse before any further move was attempted.

When all suspicion had been quieted, Dragut collected the troops he had in Susa and Monester, and one dark night appeared at the foot of the tower commanded by Barat. The sally-port was thrown open, and Dragut led his men through it into the tower, and thence into the town—advancing to the principal points, and taking up commanding positions, without exciting any alarm. Morning showed the citizens the misfortunes that had befallen them. With desperate resolution they ran to arms; but all was confusion, and, as is usual in such cases, they fought with more impetuosity than conduct. The corsairs had the advantage of discipline and coolness ; and after a number of citizens were killed, the rest were compelled to lay down their arms, and acknowledge for their sovereign a man whom, but a short time before, they had refused to receive as a citizen.

Additional troops were brought into the town; the several towers all strongly garrisoned, and the authority of the corsair so firmly established, that no hope remained to the citizens of the recovery of their liberty. Dragut having put the fortifications in complete order, and filled the magazines and arsenals, appointed his nephew, young Rais Essé, to the command of the garrison, while he himself departed on a cruize. His parting injunction to the young governor is eminently illustrative of the character of a Turkish corsair.

"That Moor, Barat, is a dangerous man," whispered Dragut. "You must see that he is properly disposed of."

"He let us into the city," said Rais Essé, looking at his uncle inquiringly.

"He did so," replied Dragut, demurely stroking his long black beard. "He is a terrible traitor to this good city of ours. You must see to it that he does not betray it again."

The young rais passed his hand around his throat. Dragut replied with a grave nod.

"Your will is law," exclaimed his nephew. "It shall be done."

A few hours afterwards Dragut's streamers disappeared in the distant horizon; and that night the Moor Barat went to sup with the rais, and was choked to death—whether by a bone or a bow-string could not be accurately ascertained.

CHAPTER IV.

The news of the taking of Mahedia gave great uneasiness to the emperor, as well as to all the towns on the northern shores of the Mediterranean. Charles saw plainly that Dragut's power, already formidable, would be vastly increased by the possession of so strong a naval depot, to which he could retreat with his prizes, and from whence he could annoy, almost with impunity, the coasts of Naples and Sicily. To prevent this the emperor resolved to besiege the place without delay, before the corsair had time to settle himself more firmly in it. The enterprise, however, was acknowledged to be difficult, and it was decided in council that the best way of beginning it would be to retake possession of Susa and Monester, from whence the corsairs drew their supplies.

D'Oria was ordered immediately to sea with a powerful fleet, which was further strengthened by the Pope's galleys, and by several galleys of Malta. One hundred and forty experienced knights, under the command of the Balif de la Sangle, and a battalion of four hundred of the common soldiers of the Order, constituted the strength of the reinforcement. The Spanish admiral got under way, and stood over to the African shore, expecting, upon information he had received, to find Dragut at Monester. But the experienced corsair was not to be caught so easily a second time. He knew better than to shut himself up in so weak a place, and had taken to the open sea. Knowing that D'Oria had not troops enough on board to establish the siege of so strong a place as Mahedia, he gave himself no concern about the Spanish admiral's proceedings, but stood over to the defenceless coasts of Spain, where he committed his usual ravages. Town after town was attacked and sacked; and many an unfortunate captive had reason to regret an expedition which had drawn the Christian fleets so far from their own coasts.

In the meanwhile D'Oria, following the orders of the imperial council, landed his troops at Cape Bon, seized upon Kalibia, the ancient Aspis or Clypea, and thence advanced to the gates of Monester. The inhabitants encouraged by the small number of his troops, made a sally, mainly for the purpose of reconnoitering. They were charged vigorously by the Knights of Malta, and compelled to come to an engagement, when they were routed, and followed so closely that the Christians entered the gates with them, and made themselves masters of the town. The remainder of the garrison and citizens took refuge in the castle.

D'Oria summoned the governor to surrender, and upon his refusal, erected his batteries and opened a fire upon the fort. As soon as a breach appeared, D'Oria, without waiting to examine it, ordered an assault. This precipitation led to the loss of many lives, especially among the knights who led the attack. The governor of the castle was a sturdy old corsair; and had he not been killed in the breach by a musket ball, after the battle had raged for an hour and a half, the assailants would have been defeated. As it was, the Christians suffered terribly, and of the knights nearly all were killed or wounded.

Costly as was this conquest of one little castle, it was looked upon by the emperor as an omen of success, and D'Oria was ordered to make every preparation for the siege of Dragut's stronghold at Mahedia. The viceroys of Naples and Sicily were ordered to supply men and ammunition.

While waiting for the reinforcements which they were to send, D'Oria removed his fleet to an anchorage among some little islands in the neighborhood of Mahedia, in order to prevent Dragut from throwing any additional force into the town; but his design was frustrated by the necessity of attending the viceroy of Sicily, Don Juan de Vega, who had written to him that he was getting ready a strong force which, considering the interest that Sicily had in the destruction of the corsairs, he was determined to command in person. But as it would take some time before all his preparations could be finished, and as Dragut was scouring the seas with several squadrons, in order to surprise the Christian vessels, and ruin the enterprise, he insisted that the admiral should appoint the general rendezvous of the fleets at Drepano, from whence the united sea forces of the emperor could sail without fear of having any of their transports and store-ships picked up by the indefatigable Dragut.

D'Oria was exceedingly chagrined to be compelled to give up the blockade of Mahedia; but Don Juan was an experienced officer, and a great favorite with the emperor, and the admiral's private orders were to do nothing in the matter of the siege without his advice. The admiral was compelled to weigh anchor, and proceed to Palermo; whence, in company with Juan de Vega, he sailed to Drepano, at which place he found the armaments of Naples and Malta waiting his arrival.

Every reader of history has noticed what an important part petty official vanity—the mere jealousy of rank—has frequently played in the affairs of the world. It would be difficult to enumerate a tithe of the well laid plans which have been thwarted, or the military and naval expeditions which have been defeated, solely from divisions and disagreements on the most trivial questions of rank and precedence. So true is this, that the jealousies of generals is an element which must not be neglected, even in the present day, in estimating the probability of any military success. D'Oria found, to his great grief, upon his arrival at Drepano, that this element demanded his whole attention.

The Neapolitan troops, consisting of twenty-four galleys, and several transports, with land troops, were commanded by Don Garcia, son of Don Pedro de Toledo, viceroy of Naples. This young man had flattered himself with the hope of being sole commander of the land forces, and of having the whole conduct of the siege. When he found that the viceroy of Sicily had resolved to command the reinforcements he brought with him in person, young Garcia reëmbarked his troops, resolving to go on a separate expedition against Dragut, rather than share the honors of a command with his equal in rank, and his superior in age and renown.

The admiral found the greatest difficulty in reconciling the pretensions of the two haughty dons; but at length, after several days negotiations, in which De la Sangle, the commander of the Maltese, took an active part, the affair was settled. It was arranged that each should retain command of his own troops independent of the other, and that a council of war should represent the imperial name, and determine, by a majority of voices, the operations of the siege.

Dragut, in the meantime, had not been idle. A strong reinforcement was thrown into the town, commanded by some of his best officers, and every preparation made for a stout defence. He himself remained at sea, ready to pounce upon any straggling galleys, intercept supplies, and in every possible way interfere with the operations of the besiegers.

It is quite probable that not a dozen readers of this sketch have ever heard of Mahedia, or of this famous siege; but at the time the eyes of all Europe were drawn towards it, and men listened with a degree of anxiety proportioned to their fears of the arch corsair, for news of the capture and destruction of his stronghold. In consideration of the former interest in the subject, and the present ignorance of the general reader in relation to it, we may be excused for abridging from the historians of the period an account of the principal events of the expedition.

Without opposition or difficulty D'Oria landed his troops and artillery. The city was invested, trenches opened, batteries mounted, and a fire opened upon the walls. The magistrates and principal citizens of the town, seeing the strength of the Spanish forces, and not being any too well satisfied with the government of the corsair, were disposed to capitulate, but young Rais Essé drove all such thoughts from their heads with the point of his dagger.

"Dare to mention the word capitulate again," exclaimed the resolute rover, flourishing his weapon, "and I will stab you with my own hand, and then set fire to the city. To capitulate would be your destruction. Think you that the Christians would leave you the exercise of your religion, and the enjoyment of your wealth? Fools as well as cowards! Everything that is dear to you is at stake. You must fight for your lives—your religion—your wives and children, and property."

The rais went on to encourage their hopes of a successful resistance; pointing out the strength of the town, and telling them that he had a force of seventeen hundred foot and six hundred horse, with which, in conjunction with their aid, he felt confident of making a good defence. The magistrates silenced, but not convinced, were forced to submit; but the populace, urged by religious zeal, sided readily with the rais. To confirm their enthusiasm, he ordered a sortie of cavalry, supported by three hundred arquebusiers and some light field pieces. The sallying party advanced to a rising ground, and opened a spirited fire upon the Christians. Don Garcia, whose quarters lay nearest, rushed with a part of his force to dislodge them from their position, when a warm and obstinate skirmish ensued. The rais despatched six hundred men to the support of troops, who, thus reinforced, made terrible havoc among the Neapolitans. The viceroy De Vega was not sorry to see the young don receive such a check; but he could not quietly stand by and permit the Neapolitan soldiers to be entirely destroyed. The soldiers of Malta, with La Sangle at their head, were despatched to the rescue. Their presence turned the tide of battle. Sword in hand, they charged the Moors, who, unable to withstand the disciplined impetuosity of the veteran soldiers of the cross, broke and fled; the infantry getting back into town, and the cavalry galloping away across the plain to a forest of olives, in which they disappeared.

As soon as a breach appeared in the wall running across the land side, the viceroy determined upon an assault, notwithstanding the unfavorable report of the engineers, who announced that within the breach were strong entrenchments, well flanked and defended. He, however, fancying the reports to be exaggerated, persuaded his officers to appoint the ensuing Friday for the assault; and in the interval the fire of the battery was redoubled, in order to widen the breach. On Friday, two hours before daybreak, the viceroy, who was for having all the honor of the enterprise to himself, advanced with his own troops to the foot of the wall, notwithstanding the undisputed right of the knights to head all attacks.

The assault was most unfortunate. The Sicilians advanced with courage, and were received with a terrible fire, despite of which they pushed up to the top of the breach, and gallantly threw themselves over into the ditch between the wall and the inner intrenchments. Here a flanking fire swept them down, until but a single man remained, whose life was spared in order to obtain from him some information of the designs of the Christians. Other troops advanced to the support of those in the breach; but with no better success. Already many of the bravest men had perished, and the generals, to prevent the loss of any more, were compelled to order a retreat.

The ardor of the besiegers was very much dampened by the result of this assault. The dejected soldiery did not dare to speak of raising the siege, but they saw plainly enough that it would take a long time; and already their provisions were beginning to fail, and camp fevers to show themselves. Luckily the Knights of Malta were present. In obedience to the orders and example of La Sangle, they established hospitals in their tents, and nursed the sick soldiers with unremitting attention and kindness.

The circumstances which had depressed the besiegers gave additional confidence to the soldiers of the garrison; and their spirits were still further raised by the safe arrival of two stout swimmers, bearing letters from

Dragut, in which he announced his landing on the coast a few miles to the west, with eight hundred men, and his intention of attempting to surprise the Christians in camp on St. James' day, when he supposed their watchfulness would be relaxed by the usual festivities of the occasion.

Pursuant to this well laid plan, Dragut secreted himself in a spacious forest of olive trees, not far from the town. Luckily for the Christians, they were in the habit of visiting this wood almost daily, for fuel and fascines, and chance brought on an engagement sooner than Dragut had proposed. In this forest there was an old summer palace of Mahedi, the founder of the city, and it was from one of its turrets that Dragut was reconnoitering the Christian camp, when he saw an unusually strong detachment issue forth, and take up its line of march towards him. Some suspicion had been excited in the minds of certain renegade Moors serving in the Christian camp, by the uncommon boldness of the country people in advancing to skirmish; and although the Spanish officers had no apprehension of Dragut's presence, it was thought prudent to visit the wood in stronger force than usual. The viceroy led the detachment in person, and La Sangle accompanied it with his knights.

Dragut kept quiet until the Christians were almost upon him, when suddenly pouring in a volley of musketry, he rushed out and charged the Christians sword in hand. The surprise was complete, and with any other soldiers than the famous Knights of Malta would have been most disastrous. These sturdy old warriors did not allow their ranks to fall into confusion. They formed their lines steadily, and received Dragut's charge without wavering. The conflict was long, obstinate, and bloody. Dragut's Moorish auxiliaries—two or three thousand in number—coming up, the viceroy had great difficulty in withdrawing his troops from the wood, and regaining the plain, where he was followed by Dragut, who, however, finding that no further advantage was to be gained, ordered a retreat. While this was going on, the camp was also a scene of confusion. Upon hearing the news of the battle in the forest, Rais Essé issued from the city, penetrated the Christian lines, and attacked Don Garcia, who was in command. The young nobleman behaved with great coolness and prudence; but it was only after a desperate conflict that he compelled the corsairs to retreat within the gates.

The prospects of the besiegers were now of the most gloomy description. The batteries kept up a continued fire; but the walls were so thick and the breaches so small, and so well guarded by interior entrenchments, that the council of war did not dare to order another assault. On the contrary, the question of raising the siege began to be agitated. To this movement no officer was so strongly opposed as the young and enthusiastic Don Garcia. Greedy of glory, his high spirit could ill bear the idea of taking back to the vice-regal court of Naples nothing but the shame of defeat. "Never!" he exclaimed energetically to the Neapolitan officers, "will I consent to such dishonor; sooner will I lay my bones in these trenches. But, fear not, the saints will yet befriend us—that is, if we keep our batteries playing vigorously. I feel a presentiment that a way through those walls will shortly be opened to us."

"Perhaps," replied an officer who had just entered the tent, "here is one who can inform your excellency where the opening is to be made. He is a Moresco—a deserter from the town. He says that he has valuable information, which he will communicate only to the commander-in-chief."

The Moor was admitted; when to Don Garcia's questions he replied that a detestation of the corsairs, and a desire to see them driven out of the city, had induced him to seek the Spanish commander, and point out a place in the walls where a breach could be made with effect.

The spot indicated as being much weaker than the rest was a portion of the wall washed by the sea, which had been neglected by the garrison, under the idea that the sand bars would prevent any vessels from approaching it. Don Garcia's plans were instantly formed. Taking two old flat-bottomed hulks, he covered them with a platform, mounted his guns, and shoved this floating battery up to within breaching distance of the wall. In a few hours, such was the rapidity and force of the fire, a practicable breach was made, and an assault ordered.

No precautions this time were wanting. The Knights of Malta, pursuant to custom and the privilege of that illustrious order, had the post of honor assigned them, and advanced to the storm. The commander Giou, supported by two files of the oldest knights, bore the standard of the cross. Following him came the chivalrous Guimeran and Copier, with the younger knights and volunteers. Four companies of the Maltese battalion, with La Sangle, and a few of the oldest knights, brought up the rear of this gallant storming party.

To distract the attention of the enemy, the viceroy and Don Garcia led their troops to the assault of the breaches in the land wall. A cannon shot gave the signal for the assault. The Knights of St. John advanced in light boats; but finding their progress continually impeded by sand bars, with characteristic intrepidity they leaped into the water, and waded forward, amid showers of grape-shot, musket-balls, arrows, stones, fire-pots, and boiling oil. On went the standard of the order, and up to the breach, despite the desperate resistance of the Moors, pressed its guard of grim, grizzly, war-worn veterans, followed by their more youthful companions. The top of the breach was gained. De Giou was at the moment struck by a musket ball; but the sacred banner was instantly seized by Copier, and supported steadily aloft, above the tumult of the fight—a mark for a furious storm of musketry and crossbow shot. The situation of the knights was now eminently critical. It was impossible to advance any further, or to reach the Moors, who had retreated to their entrenchments. The cannon from the neighboring tower increased the havoc making in their ranks. Many of the best knights had fallen. Still there was no flinching—no movement towards a retreat. With the utmost coolness they sought for some passage through the ruins. At length De Guimeran discovered the entrance to a ruined gallery, leading into the body of the place. Loud rose again the battle-cry of the order. "Ho! for St. John! and down with the Infidel!" shouted the knights, as they forced their way towards the gallery. Again a terrible hand to hand struggle took place; but onward, onward, surging and swaying, but ever advancing, the compact band worked its way over the ruins. The Moors are driven aside, or cut down and trampled under foot. The knights reach the entrance of the gallery. De Guimeran leads the way, and rushes across the broken joists and beams with as much resolution as he would have done over a stone bridge. His companions lag not behind; with irresistable impulse they burst through all further defences; and the standard of St. John waves within the doomed city.

As usual in such cases, a panic took place among the citizens. The defences of the city were deserted, and over them poured the troops of the viceroy and Don Garcia. The Moors took refuge in their houses and public buildings, from whence they kept up a desperate resistance. But it availed not; the indomitable knights pressed them from point to point—drove them from the castle and custom house, and finally forced them to lay down their arms and beg for their lives. Ten thousand captives, and an immense booty, rewarded the gallantry of the victors. Among the captives was the gallant young rais, who, until he was ransomed by his uncle, had to expiate the sin of defeat at the oar of a Maltese galley.*

* The reader may, perhaps, be curious as to the final fate of this fine city, which so narrowly missed becoming, under Dragut, the capital of a flourishing piratical state; if so, see Appendix for an extract from Marmol's Africa, translated by Morgan for his quaint old history of Algiers.

CHAPTER V.

The rage and mortification of Dragut may be imagined when he learned that his newly established stronghold had yielded to the fiery ardor of the knights, and that with it had fled his well-founded hopes of sovereign power.

"The knights! the knights!" exclaimed the enraged corsair, pulling his beard with one hand, and shaking the other in the direction of the island. "The knights! May the curse of the Prophet rest upon the rock they inhabit! They are the cause of it all. Without them, not a Christian eye had dared look at the bastions of Mahedia. But I will have revenge."

"Aye, aye," replied one of a group of excited Turks gathered on the quarter-deck of the admiral's galley; "we will sweep up their wheat vessels from Sicily."

"More than that!" fiercely replied Dragut.

"We will drive their galleys from the sea," continued the speaker.

"More than that," rejoined Dragut. "Aye, by my beard, and by the beard of the Prophet, I will crush the dogs in their kennel. And to that end I commit these letters for our lord the sultan to your care, Rais Harré. You have a swift galley: up anchor, and away with all speed to Constantinople. Deliver them to the grand signior yourself. Say to him that the loss of Mahedia is not mine. Tell him that these knights must be driven from Malta, as they were from Rhodes; that they are the tools of Spain, and without them, the great enemy of our faith, Charles, would be powerless. See to it, rais, and bring me the favorable decision of our master. And," continued Dragut, drawing the rais aside, "see that the hinges of the Porte are well oiled. For that purpose here are bills on the Armenians for one hundred thousand ducats; and here is a memorandum of the proportions in which they are to be applied."

In obedience to his directions the rais got his galley in motion, and made his way with all speed to Constantinople. The arguments and money of Dragut had a powerful influence; and soon the rumor began to spread throughout the Mediterranean of an extraordinary degree of activity in the Turkish arsenals and dockyards. Preparations for war on so grand a scale could not long be concealed, although for awhile it was doubtful upon what quarter of christendom the storm would burst.

Dragut was known to be chief mover in the whole affair. It was his energy, his money, and his personal influence that were threatening the emperor with a war to which he was but ill disposed. Charles and his advisers imagined that if they could get the arch corsair once more in their power, that Suleiman, deprived of his most able and energetic officer, would be disposed to peace.

Orders were accordingly issued to D'Oria to proceed to sea with all the force he could collect, and once more seek out Dragut, and either capture or destroy him. With twenty-two royal galleys, besides numerous smaller vessels, the imperial admiral set sail for the coast of Africa, and had the good fortune to make a rapid run.

Dragut was lying at this time at port in the little island off Jerba, situated on the African coast, about midway between Tripoli and Tunis. It was so early in the season—the month of March—that he did not dream of the appearance of an enemy in force. His own galleys were partly disarmed, while leisurely refitting for the spring cruise.

Not a little astonished and mortified was the experienced corsair when the imperial fleet suddenly showed itself off the mouth of the harbor, and he found himself caught in a trap similar to the one into which he had fallen on the coast of Corsica. At the first news of the approach of the Christians, he hurried to where he could obtain a view of them, and for a few moments, as if confounded, stood silently watching them as they came to anchor just at the entrance of the long winding port. His officers gathered around him, anxious to catch the slightest expression of hope or fear.

"Allah! what a fate awaits us!" groaned one. "We shall be all made slaves."

"Never!" exclaimed Dragut. "The Christian oar is not numbered, and never will be, to which these hands will be again attached. Come, we will show these dogs a good front. Let the galleys that are afloat sweep down to this bend of the channel, and open a fire, while the rest of you bring a few pieces of artillery to this point. We will see how they like the salute we give them."

Dragut's orders were obeyed with promptness, and soon a fire was opened upon the Christians that compelled them to raise their anchors, and take up a position further off from the shore, though still near enough to prevent all egress from the harbor. With his usual promptitude he marked out a fortification commanding the channel, and before the next morning it was complete, with its guns mounted in battery, the fire from which compelled the Spanish admiral to draw still further off. If Dragut could not get out, D'Oria could not get in, and so far they were even; although the admiral had the advantage of being able to send to Sicily for a reinforcement of land forces. While waiting the arrival of these he employed his time examining the coasts of the island, and making sure that there was no outlet except the one occupied by his fleet. He also ordered a survey of the harbor, as far as practicable, so as to enable his fleet to coöperate in the attack of the fort as soon as the Sicilian soldiers should arrive. For this purpose a light brigantine was sent in to make out the channel by stakes, with little flags affixed to them.

Dragut was at no loss to understand the meaning of the movements of the brigantine; and no sooner was her mission accomplished than he jumped into his barge, and rowed down towards the Spanish fleet, pulling up, as he passed, the channel marks so industriously planted. So rapid and energetic were his movements that, amid a shower of cannon-shot, he succeeded in undoing in a few minutes the labor of the Spaniards for several days. He also threw up new entrenchments along the banks of the harbor, furnished them with artillery, and manned them with musketeers; so that not a boat or light galley could show itself within the canal.

The Spaniards, however, could well afford to laugh

at all his precautions, knowing that when the expected troops should arrive a landing could be effected, and his batteries either turned or forced. All that was required was a little patience, and the arch corsair—the terror of the Mediterranean—the most dangerous enemy of the emperor—would be in their power.

The imperial officers were in high spirits, although somewhat weary of the monotonous blockade. Hourly they expected a message from the approaching reinforcement, and eagerly did they watch the horizon seaward for the appearance of a sail. At length their eyes were gratified by the sight of a distant galley, which gradually, as it approached, grew more and more distinct, until at last the cross on her banner showed her to be a vessel of Malta. Too impatient for her tidings to permit him to wait her approach, D'Oria jumped aboard one of his brigantines, and stood out to meet her. The galley evidently bore news of importance, which her captain was anxious to deliver. Every sail was trimmed to the light breeze, and her oars rose and fell in the water with a rapidity and energy seldom seen but in a chase. She was soon alongside, and within speaking distance of the admiral.

"What news!" demanded D'Oria.

"Bad enough," replied the captain of the galley. "I am sorry to be the bearer of such disagreeable tidings."

"Ha!" exclaimed the impatient admiral; "has anything happened to the armament of the viceroy? Madre de Dios! but that would be bad, indeed."

"Worse than that," replied the captain.

"How worse? The viceroy does not dare to refuse the troops I demand. By heavens! I care not if he does," continued D'Oria, addressing the officers around him. "We will lie here until the emperor himself comes to our assistance, or till our galleys rot at their moorings, sooner than let yonder rat out of his trap!"

"'Tis not of the viceroy that I bring bad news," said the captain, hesitating.

"Of the emperor?"

"No."

"The Virgin be praised! Perhaps of the grand master of your order?"

"Not so."

"Who, then?" demanded D'Oria impatiently, forgetting that his own interruptions prevented the captain from delivering his news.

"Of Dragut."

"What of him?"

"He is at sea with his whole force."

A smile of incredulity mantled the faces of the imperial officers; which, however, gradually subsided to a grave expression of anxiety and doubt as the Maltese continued.

"We encountered him yesterday, when we were sailing in company with the Padrona galley of Sicily, which was bringing a messenger from the viceroy. Dragut gave chase, and the Sicilian was caught. We were the fleetest; but we had a narrow escape."

"Santa Maria!" exclaimed D'Oria. "Dragut at sea? Impossible! Yonder he is, shut up with all his galleys. It must have been some squadron from the Levant, that we know nothing of."

"Not so," returned the captain. "I know Dragut's galley well. I saw his peculiar signals flying; and I heard his men, as they boarded the Sicilian, shout his battle-cry."

"And what was his force?"

"Twelve galleys, besides galliots and brigantines."

The admiral and his officers looked at each other in astonishment.

"Here is some mystification," exclaimed D'Oria—"the work of that devil yonder. He has found some way to send for a squadron of Levant corsairs, in hopes to draw us off, and give him a chance to get out of the trap. But let us weigh anchor and stand in. We will soon see if the old sea-fox is not in his hole."

The mortification of the Spanish officers may be conceived upon finding, as they moved into the harbor, that they were not received with the expected salute of cannon-shot. They were suffered quietly to advance until abreast of the bastion which Dragut had erected, when they were met by a boat with a white flag, bearing a message from the sheick of the island, proposing to capitulate, upon condition that the lives and property of the islanders should be spared.

"But Dragut! What of him?" demanded the Christians.

"Gone. Yesterday he put to sea with his whole force."

The impatient and mortified D'Oria hastened to land, when the secret of Dragut's flight was revealed. The ingenious and energetic corsair, while amusing the enemy with his bastions and batteries at the mouth of the harbor, had employed the chief part of his forces in grading a road across the island—a distance of twelve or fourteen miles. Upon this road he laid down a track of wooden rails, and then, by means of capstans and pullies, drew his vessels up from the water into cradles, with rollers attached to them, and shoving them across the island, dropped them into a canal leading to the sea, which he had dug to receive them. So adroitly had he masked his work, that the Spaniards had not the slightest suspicion of what was going on. When all was prepared he shipped his crews, and launched out into the open sea, picking up the Padrone galley almost within sight of the imperial fleet, and then steering a course for the coasts of Spain.

No event in that age of striking events produced a greater sensation than this dexterous escape of the great corsair. The reputation of Dragut was at its height, and all Europe, from Constantinople to Cadiz, was filled with his renown. The Spanish admiral, completely confounded by the turn affairs had taken, set sail for Genoa, after apprising the viceroys of Naples and Sicily that Dragut was at large, and warning them against exposing single galleys or small squadrons to the danger of capture. To excuse himself from an enterprise so liable to failure as the further pursuit of Dragut, D'Oria, it is said, "made use of the honorable pretext of commanding in person the galleys appointed to conduct from Italy the emperor's only son, afterwards Philip II," of Spain.

CHAPTER VI.

At liberty once more to prosecute his plans for revenge upon the Knights of St. John, Dragut repaired to Constantinople to superintend in person the preparation of the expedition which his representations and solicitations had induced the grand signior to commence. The Ottoman armada was soon in readiness, and, under the command of Sinan, captain-basha, sailed from the Dardanelles, with instructions to attack Malta if it should be judged prudent; otherwise, to proceed to Tripoli, then a possession of the Order. Although not in command of the expedition, such was the sultan's confidence in Dragut's judgment and knowledge, that the strictest orders were issued to Sinan to take no step of importance without his advice.

In July, 1551, the Turkish fleet came within sight of Malta. The captain-basha and his officers were strongly in favor of proceeding at once to Tripoli, without making any demonstration against the island; but

Dragut insisted so strenuously upon landing, that Sinan did not dare refuse. The indisposition of Sinan, however, to an energetic prosecution of the siege was openly manifested. Upon reconnoitering the castle of St. Angelo, he turned angrily to Dragut, and exclaimed, "Is this the castle you have represented to the grand signior as so easy to be taken? No eagle could have chosen a less accessible rock to build his nest upon."

"And yonder bastion," exclaimed one of the surrounding group of officers. "Do you see it, my lord? That upon which the knights have planted their grand standard. You must know, my lord, that when I was a slave here I assisted in carrying all the great stones of which it is built; and certain I am, that before we can batter it down, the winter will be upon us, or, still worse, powerful reinforcements, for these dogs will arrive."

With a look of indignant surprise Dragut exclaimed: "Who dares talk of failure? The castle of St. Angelo is strong—I never denied it; but it can be taken, and it is worth any risk or expense. If we take it, we shall capture the grand master and all his knights, as in a net; when we can crush them like so many flies."

Sinan, however, and his officers had too lively an apprehension of the difficulties of the enterprise. They knew that it was not so much the strength of the works as the valor of their defenders that they had to fear, and, besides, were not urged on by the personal motives which actuated Dragut. Still, their instructions would not permit them to disregard his wishes entirely, and, as a compromise, they agreed to attack La Citta Notabile, the ancient capital of the island, in which the greater part of the natives had taken refuge with their effects. This city was accordingly invested; but the defence was so vigorous, and the Turks so ill disposed to the attack, and so much disturbed by rumors of the arrival of D'Oria with a powerful fleet, that it was resolved to abandon the siege, despite the entreaties of Dragut to the contrary.

The Turks left the island after plundering and burning several villages, and proceeded to the neighboring island of Goza, a dependency of Malta. The castle was commanded by the Chevalier Galatian de Sessa, who evinced a degree of fear never before exhibited by a Knight of St. John. He actually deserted the walls, and secreted himself in the lower rooms of the castle. Many weary years of captivity was the fitting punishment of his cowardice; involving as it did the lives and liberties of the unhappy islanders, more than six thousand of whom were carried away captives.

From Goza the fleet sailed to Tripoli; Dragut's reluctance at leaving Malta being somewhat appeased by the prospect of inflicting a severe injury upon his enemies, and securing a stronghold for himself by the reduction of that place.

Our space will not permit a description of the siege; which would not be, however, if we had room for it, unaccompanied by many details of interest. Suffice it to say, that the defence was conducted with resolution, under the command of the Marshal de Villier, but that incited and aided by the example and advice of the indefatigable Dragut, the siege was pushed with so much vigor that the Christians were compelled to surrender.

Dragut was appointed governor; when he at once set about rebuilding the fortifications, adding new works, and putting the city in a position to resist the efforts which he knew his enemies would soon make for its recapture. But while engaged in this work he did not neglect his ordinary duties. His expeditions to all parts of the Mediterranean were frequent and destructive. Many towns were plundered and burned, thousands of Christians carried into captivity, and numerous valuable prizes taken at sea.

The Knights of St. John had at this time elected the renowned Lavellet grand master of their order. Under his wise and energetic government the fortification of the island, which had been much neglected by his predecessors, were strengthened, and many new works built. The knights were in high spirits at the successful prosecution of these defences, when an event occurred which for a while dampened their spirits. A hurricane, of which there had been hardly a minute's warning, burst with irresistable fury upon the island. Most of the galleys in port were overturned and destroyed, and more than six hundred persons—among whom were many knights of distinction—lost their lives.

The storm had hardly cleared away when Dragut's squadron was seen off the coast. The energetic old corsair had hastened to take advantage of the misfortunes of his enemies, and had come to pay them a visit in their defenceless condition. He landed his forces, plundered and destroyed several villages, and made many slaves. He was not, however, permitted to escape unharmed. Three hundred knights, followed by the native militia of the island, attacked his troops so vigorously, that it was with considerable difficulty that he managed to retreat with his spoil.

The danger of allowing Dragut to establish himself firmly in his new possession at length aroused the imperial court to action, and an expedition against Tripoli was resolved upon. Philip II sent orders to the governor of the Milanese, to the governor of Naples, and to John Andrea D'Oria, to join their forces to those of the viceroy of Sicily, and the grand master of Malta, for this purpose. Upon hearing, however, of the new fortifications which Dragut had erected, the ardor of the viceroy suffered an abatement, and he proposed that, instead of attacking Tripoli, their arms should be directed against the island of Gelves. As this would be to abandon the main object of the expedition, it was strongly opposed by the grand master, who declared his intention of withdrawing his knights in case the design was persisted in. This disagreement was for awhile patched up, upon the promise of the viceroy to proceed at once against Tripoli; but it was an omen of the troubles which attended the whole of the ill-fated expedition. The viceroy had not the courage to keep his promise. After losing several vessels by a storm in the neighborhood of Tripoli, the course of the fleet was changed for the island of Gelves, which, formerly independent, had become a tributary to Dragut. A landing was effected without difficulty. An attack by the natives was vigorously repulsed, and the governor compelled to surrender his castle.

Intoxicated by this easy success, the viceroy boasted that he was the first general who had done anything towards enlarging the dominions of his master the king of Spain; and in order to retain his conquest, he resolved to build a fort which should defy the efforts of the Moors. The prosecution of this work led to great delays; sickness broke out in the camp; D'Oria was taken ill, and numbers were carried to the grave. At length a powerful Turkish fleet appeared, and the ruin of the unfortunate expedition was complete. The Turks took twenty galleys and fourteen transports, while others were sunk or lost on the flats. A few escaped, and among them were three galleys of Malta, and the galley of the Spanish admiral.

The discomfiture of the Christians far from satisfied the vengeance of the great corsair. His efforts were again directed towards exciting the Ottoman court to a new expedition against the knights. He was warmly seconded by Hassan, basha of Algiers, and the son and successor of the famous Barbarossa; by whom it was urged that the knights were the most dangerous foes of the Turks, and that the communication between Barbary and Constantinople would ultimately be cut off entirely, unless this nest of Christian pirates was destroyed.

Suleiman was sensible of the importance of this conquest; but as it might be attended with difficulties, he resolved to proceed with caution, and to take no step without consulting his generals. For this purpose he called a grand council of war on horseback. Dragut's agent, who was present, represented that it would be the safest course of proceeding to reduce the fortress held by Spain in Barbary, from whence the knights could draw succors, and then attack the island. In this opinion he was supported by Mohammed Basha, the oldest and most experienced of the Turkish generals, but Suleiman himself was in favor of commencing with Malta; and a majority of his courtiers, with the usual servility of their kind, supported his views.

Again did the Christian world resound with rumors of the vast armaments preparing in the Turkish ports. Nothing was known with certainty as to their precise destination; but the general opinion seemed to point out the Knights of St. John as the intended victims. Luckily, these gallant soldiers of the cross had in John de La Valette, a grand master admirably adapted to the exigencies of the occasion. His courage and confidence rose as the imminence and extent of the danger manifested itself; and he had the happy art of infusing his own spirit into the breasts of his companions. Upon receiving positive advices in relation to the designs of the Turks, he assembled his knights, and addressed them.

"A formidable army," said he, "and an infinite multitude of barbarians, are coming to thunder down upon us: they are, my brethren, enemies to Jesus Christ. It is our business to stand up manfully in defence of the faith; and if the Gospel must submit to the Koran, God demands back of us a life which we have already devoted to him by our profession. Thrice happy they who shall first fall a sacrifice in so good a cause. But in order to make ourselves worthy of that honor, let us go, my brethren, to the altar, there to renew our vows and partake of the blessed sacraments; and let the blood of the Saviour of mankind inspire us with such a noble contempt of death, as can alone make us invincible."

A lively and refreshing sentiment of devotion and faith pervaded all ranks. Several days were employed in religious services—in going to confession, and in partaking of the eucharist—rising up, as the Abbe Vertot says, "from the Lord's table like new men. All their weaknesses were repaired; all divisions, all resentments were now laid aside; and what was still more difficult, they broke off all their tender engagements, so dear to the heart of man."

On the 18th of May, 1665, the Turkish fleet, consisting of one hundred and fifty-nine galleys, besides transports, bearing thirty thousand janizaries, spahis, and other land troops, appeared off the coast. A landing was effected; and, after much hesitation and several skirmishes, the fort of St. Elmo was selected as the principal point of attack.

The trenches were opened, and batteries mounted; when Dragut, with fifteen vessels and sixteen hundred men, arrived upon the scene. He immediately expressed his regret at their having commenced the siege with St. Elmo; but when the Turkish generals offered to alter their plan of operations in deference to his judgment, he replied that it would be dishonorable to the sultan's arms, and disheartening to the soldiers, to abandon the trenches already opened. Throwing himself with his usual energy into the work, he exerted himself day and night to encourage the soldiers and forward the siege. He superintended the mounting of the batteries, and in person pointed the guns. Wherever there was the most danger, there was Dragut.

The fort of St. Elmo was in ruins, and it was resolved to hazard a general assault. Dragut, reckless of danger, advanced beyond the protection of the epaulment, for the purpose of reconnoitering the ground, when a shot from the castle of St. Angelo dashed a stone to fragments, one of which struck him on the side of the head, and felled him senseless to the ground, with the blood streaming from his mouth, nose, and ears. Mustapha Basha, the general-in-chief of the Turks, rushed out of the trenches, and threw a carpet over him, in order to conceal the disheartening sight from the soldiers, and then caused him to be taken to his tent, when he was found still living.

A vigorous assault the next day was successfully resisted. It was renewed again two days after; and nowhere in the voluminous annals of war is there to be found a record of more desperate and unflinching valor. The Turks persisted, at a loss of eight thousand men, in forcing their way into the fort; but they entered only over the dead bodies of its brave defenders. Not a single knight was left alive to man the breach. The basha is said to have exclaimed, with reference to the smallness of the work, and the probable difficulty they would have with the town, "What will not the father cost us, when the son, who is so small, has cost us the bravest of our soldiers?"

The news of the reduction of the fort was carried to Dragut, who had recovered his sense, but not his speech. He received it with evident signs of satisfaction; when lifting his eyes towards heaven, as if in thanksgiving, he suddenly expired.

Thus ended the career of one of the most extraordinary men of his age. A man whose name, now forgotten, was once one to conjure with in every town on both sides of the Mediterranean. Few men ever equalled him in all the qualities of a great commander; no one ever surpassed him in courage, in presence of mind, or in perseverance. The historians praise even his humanity; not that he was particularly kind in his treatment of his captives—the customs of the age, as well among Christians as among Turks and Moors, would have prevented that—but he never treated them with wanton cruelty. The circumstances of his birth, his profession and his creed, were all against him; but still he managed to put himself clearly and decidedly within the category of great men. Had he been born to a throne, he would unquestionably have divided the page of history with his great and powerful enemy, Charles the Fifth.

It is not the purpose of this sketch to give the details of the famous siege in which Dragut perished. If the reader is anxious to know with what desperate energy the Turks persisted in the attack, and with what indomitable resolution and courage the knights resisted, until, after immense losses on both sides, the besiegers were compelled to embark the remnant of their forces, leaving the defences of Malta in ruins, but its gallant defenders unsubdued, he has only to refer to any one of the thousand histories of Charles and his times.

THE

PIOUS CONSTANCY

OF

INEZ DE MENCIA MONT-ROY.

CHAPTER I.

In the year 1536 the town of Agadeer, situated in Soos, the most southerly province of the kingdom of Morocco, on the coast of the Atlantic, was in possession of the Portuguese. It was deemed an exceedingly strong place, having good defences—natural and artificial—a numerous garrison, an able and resolute commander, and having frequently withstood the assaults of the surrounding Moors.

It was one bright, balmy morning of that year, that a young girl of singular beauty threw open the door of a small turret leading on to the flat roof of the governor's house. She was habited in a loose gown of white linen, girded to her waist by a silken Moorish sash. A black mantilla was thrown carelessly, with flowing ends, over her dark hair, which, braided in many strands, was looped up in long pendant folds, and secured by ribbons to a silver comb. Loose slippers of yellow Morocco partially covered her small, plump and stockingless feet. Her figure was slight, but round; her face of a perfect oval; her complexion dark, but of wonderful purity; and her eyes so large and black, with so mild and dreamy an expression, and yet with so many indications of latent passion and power, that no one upon whom they fell could resist their influence. As she appeared alone on the terrace for her usual morning walk, the distant sentinels on the ramparts commanding a view over the battlements of the house involuntarily raised their hands in salute, and drawing themselves up, strutted off on their rounds with a more stately step, as if immediately under the eye of the fair being in whom they recognised the only daughter of their governor, Donna Inez de Mencia Mont-Roy.

Inez had just risen from her devotions; and the elevated expression of pure and pious feeling yet lingered on her countenance, harmonizing admirably with the scene around: the pure sky above, tinged with the golden light of early morning; the magnificent peaks of the Atlas gleaming in the level sunbeams; and below her, the broad deep blue expanse of the quiet ocean.

For a few moments she seemed to surrender herself to the general influence of the view; but anon her eyes settled, with a look of peculiar interest, upon a grove of straggling cork trees just beyond the walls, which had been suffered to trench upon the slope of the glacis. Nothing appeared to repay the glances of the fair Inez, and with a faint half-breathed sigh she turned, and commenced pacing the terrace; gradually extending her walk, until, unconsciously, she entered a slender gallery forming a communication with the rampart of a bastion which projected towards the grove. There was nothing strange in this; she had done it a hundred times before. The bastion was secluded, only a single sentinel appearing within sight, and the gallery had been thrown across on purpose to convert it into a quiet and private promenade. But somehow this time there was a hesitation in her step that she herself would have been puzzled to explain. Onward, however, she went, until she reached the parapet of the bastion; when stepping upon the banquette, she leaned her arms upon the wall, and looked over on to the narrow glacis.

Again her keen glance penetrated the grove of cork trees—and this time not in vain; for suddenly there appeared a figure habited in Moorish garb, and mounted on a large powerful horse of superb action. The animal and his rider seemed to Donna Inez's eyes to spring from the ground with two or three vigorous bounds. The next instant the action of the animal was arrested, and his rider sat motionless for awhile within the shelter of the wood. Then dismounting, he fastened his horse to a tree, and drawing his haick over his head, sauntered carelessly out on the open glacis towards the foot of the bastion.

The first impulse of Inez was to retreat to the terrace; but she would not admit to herself that there could be anything in the appearance of a wandering Moor outside of the walls of the town to disturb her, and simply drawing the folds of her mantilla around her face, she awaited with a beating heart his gradual and indirect approach. The Moor advanced until he reached the edge of the ditch at the foot of the bastion, when, throwing back his haick, he exposed a youthful face of striking beauty. Fine regular features, and a clear light olive complexion, were admirably set off by a white turban and black curling moustach and beard. The expression of his face was also very fine, with the exception of an occasional fiery gleam of the eyes, evidently indicating, to a close observer, a latent element of ferocity in the composition of his character.

Inez started, but not with surprise; for, to tell the truth, she was not wholly unprepared to recognise in the young man before her the person of the shereef Mohammed, the master of Soos and the whole southern portion of the kingdom of Morocco.

But a week had elapsed since she had accompanied her father to a conference with the young shereef, where the terms of a truce had been arranged between the garrison and the surrounding Moors. A single glance at the unveiled face of Donna Inez had fired the heart of the inflammable Moor; while his fine face and figure, and noble air, had left an impression upon the mind of the young girl, which had for several mornings been recalled by the appearance of a mysterious horseman in the distant wood.

Inez felt the blood mount to her cheeks and brow, and she drew her mantilla closer around her face. She felt her heart beat and her limbs tremble, and she thought how wrong it would be to hold any communication with her father's enemy, and the enemy of her faith. She was about to retreat; but maiden pride withheld her. "Why should she? What was it to her that a Moor showed himself outside of the walls of the town? What right had she to suppose that his movements had anything to do with her? And was there not a truce? Had not her father and the shereef become friends?"

This reasoning was perfectly conclusive; but despite of it Inez was turning to withdraw, when her movements were arrested by the voice of the shereef.

"One moment, fair lady," he exclaimed imploringly, "just one moment, to permit me to say that upon the slightest sign I will retire instantly. I would not interrupt your morning musings. You need not fear me —I am no enemy; and if I were, is not this chasm between us?"

"Nay," returned Inez, "I have no fear; but it is unseemly for me to parley thus with my father's foe."

"Do not call me a foe," replied Mohammed. "Have we not agreed to a truce, as preparatory to a final treaty of peace and friendship? Ah, if you knew how much you had to do with that truce, you would not refuse to listen to me for a moment."

"For a moment! Well, señor, for a moment I will listen. Speak quickly, for I cannot promise to remain longer."

"All Soos, fair lady, rings with the fame of your beauty."

"And is it for such an idle compliment that you detain me?" demanded Inez.

"Not so," replied the shereef. "I was going on to say that all Soos does but echo the sentiments of the lord and master of Soos."

"Worse and worse, señor," interrupted Inez. "What are the sentiments on such a subject of the lord of Soos to me?"

"Not much, perhaps, to you, but to me everything. Ah! Inez, the first flash of your beauty pierced my breast, as with a dagger. My heart shrank and shrivelled in your careless glance, like a leaf in a furnace. I saw you but to love you. I have lived since but in the daily sight of you from those distant woods."

The impassioned look and tone of the shereef made the heart of Inez thrill with a mixed emotion of delight and fear. One moment she stood leaning over the wall to catch his words—the next, she started, and drawing back, made a movement of retreat. The young man raised his hands imploringly.

"I must retire, señor," exclaimed Inez. "Your moment is up, and I can stay here listening to your idle gallantries no longer."

"One word more, fair lady," returned Mohammed, impetuously. "I must speak now—I may not have another opportunity. I love you; how deeply, words are vain to tell. For your sake I am going to propose a treaty of perpetual peace with your countrymen; and your hand shall be the only condition I will exact. You will give your consent, lovely Inez—will you not. 'Tis for that I have sought to speak with you, before making my propositions to your father."

The strongest emotion Inez felt was astonishment at the apparent disregard of the wide religious differences separating them; but before she could find words in which to reply, the conviction rushed upon her that Mohammed's intention must be to renounce his faith, and embrace the religion of the cross. Instantly her pale cheek glowed with the flush of hope and pleasure. She saw in imagination the picture of a soul—his soul—a soul animating so noble a form—saved from the doom of the Infidel. She saw a vision of a whole nation of Infidels following the example of their prince, and yielding to the influence of the true faith. She eagerly leaned over the parapet.

"You are startled, most lovely, most enchanting Christian, by my proposal. I hope it does not displease you."

"Indeed, señor," replied Inez, "your words sound strangely from one of your faith. You forget that a Christian maiden may not listen to one whose custom it is to scoff at and revile her religion."

"But why need there be any religious differences between us?" demanded Mohammed.

"You a Christian?" replied Inez, impulsively stretching out her hand, as if to grasp the repentant Infidel, and pull him within the folds of the Church. "Thanks to the Blessed Virgin! she has heard my prayer."

"A Christian!" exclaimed Mohammed, drawing himself up proudly, while an emotion of astonishment and disgust passed across his visage. "Lady, I am a shereef—a descendant of the Prophet. The blood of Mohammed flows in these veins. Think you that I am capable not only of changing my faith, but of renouncing my lineage? Would you have me leave the path to power, and give up the grasp which I have upon the sceptre of the decaying Oataze? No, fair Inez, I would hold to all I have, if it were only to share it with thee. You can easily renounce your idolatrous creed—You are a woman—what matters your belief to you? Give it up, and, I swear to you, you shall be queen of Morocco."

The color forsook the cheek of Inez, the smile fled from her lips, as she replied: "Your sneer, señor, at a woman's faith is a fitting punishment for staying here to listen to you. I blame you not—'tis part of your creed; but know, señor, that to a Christian maiden her faith is everything: it is her only support and guide—without it she is a frail and rudderless vessel, tossed wildly upon the waves of feeling and passion, with not a chance to escape wrecking her best hopes here, to say nothing of her hopes for the next world. Señor, the religion of the blessed Jesus is a religion for woman; man may renounce it, but she can——never."

"Ah, lovely Christian!" exclaimed the shereef, "you cannot be so cruel. I will make your father intercede for me—you will think better of it in time."

"Never!" replied Inez, pulling an ivory crucifix from her bosom, and raising it to her lips. "I have been weak and foolish to parley with you so long. Adieu! And yet one word, señor: spare yourself the trouble of appealing to the Mont-Roy on such a subject. Adieu!"

The young lady drew back from the parapet, rapidly crossed the bastion and gallery, and regaining the terrace of the house, disappeared through the door of the turret. Upon reaching her apartment she dropped upon her knees before an image of the Virgin, and after acknowledging her weakness in suffering the young shereef to occupy her thoughts, she prayed for strength to resist all the temptations of passion and fancy. The act of prayer is ever its own reward; and Inez rose from her devotions calm and assured.

Not so Mohammed, who, as Inez withdrew from the parapet, stood for a while gazing at the blank wall, while a whirl of tumultuous feeling swept through his breast. His was a fiery, passionate temperament—the true temperament for a leader of fierce fanatics, the subverter of an old dynasty, and the founder of a new. He could not believe in the possibility of his suit being denied, or that Mont-Roy would let so small a matter as his daughter's religious belief interfere with the favorable reception of his propositions. "But if he should do so," he exclaimed, "I may find a way to compel his consent. These walls are not so lofty or so strong that they can long shut out the eagle of the desert."

Turning away, he regained his horse, and sprang upon his back. He threw a glance at the vacant terrace, and finding that Inez did not favor him with a parting look, passionately struck the sharp corners of his stirrup-irons into his steed, and disappeared among the trees at full gallop.

CHAPTER II.

The revolutions of Morocco had been numerous and bloody. To say nothing of the earlier ages, when Goths succeeded to Romans, and Saracens to Goths, in latter days the Almoravid dynasty, upon the defeat in Spain of Abu Hali, the grandson of the famous Yusef, who built the city of Morocco, had given way to the Almohedes. A king of this family, emulating the deeds of his great ancestor, Almansur, who defeated the Spaniards at the battle of Alarcos, had led his army across the Straits of Hercules, and on the fields of the Sierra Morena had lost two hundred thousand Moors. The political troubles consequent upon this defeat ended only with the displacement of the Almohedes, and the substitution of the Benimerini; these, in their turn, had been succeeded by the Oatazes—and it was a prince of this dynasty who was, at the period of which we write, nominally the sovereign of Morocco.

A revolution, however, had been for several years

in progress, and was at the time going on, which was destined to end in the destruction of the feeble Oataze, and the elevation to the throne of the shereefs, whose descendants have remained in power to the present day. This revolution had been commenced by Hassan, a native of Tegumedet, who pretended to be a descendant of the Prophet, and, by affecting a life of uncommon holiness and purity, had acquired great influence with the people of his province. His two sons—Hammed and Mohammed—had eagerly adopted his ambitious views, and by their energy, courage, fanaticism, and hypocrisy, had gradually worked their way to the possession of unlimited power over the provinces they had compelled the feeble king to grant them. Already the sceptre appeared within their grasp ; but mutual jealousy had prevented them for some time from extending their hands to seize it.

It was the youngest of these brothers, and the one who afterwards succeeded in deposing his sovereign, and in compelling Hammed to give up all claims to an equality of power, to whom the reader has been introduced. As he rode off, after his interview with Inez, an observer might have noticed an expression of vexation and chagrin, which sat but ill upon his handsome features. To this succeeded a look of determination. His brows were knit, his lips compressed, and his hand clenched; and then again, as he gained the open country beyond the cork trees, and spurred his horse to the top of his speed, his features relaxed into a smile of satisfaction, and an expression of confidence and hope.

The situation of the Portuguese in Africa was at this time surrounded with difficulties, arising no less from their own weakness than from the energy of their enemies. The expense of keeping up numerous garrisons upon the coast of Morocco had begun to press heavily upon the court of Lisbon; and, besides that, the attention of the whole nation had been drawn to their more important possessions in the East. It was as much, therefore, as the governor of Agadeer could do with the limited means allowed him to defend the town against the assaults of the Moors, to say nothing of protecting the people of the surrounding Berber districts, with whom his predecessors had established relations of friendship. The young shereef would not permit himself to doubt that in this condition of affairs Mont-Roy would be willing to purchase a permanent peace at the price he proposed. In truth, his idea was, that the Christian would feel himself but too highly honored by the offer. As to there being any religious scruples, he could not believe that any such would be interposed. Between men a difference of faith might be an insuperable obstacle; but in the case of a woman, it was nothing. Despite the assurances he had just received from Inez, which had astonished him for a moment, but which had failed to convince him, he felt sure that Mont-Roy would compel her at once to repeat the short formula of Mohammedan faith. As to any objections to himself personally, on the part of the maiden, Mohammed had too much confidence in his own good looks to permit him to doubt of success, even had not the instinct of passion revealed to him at a glance the admiraton he had inspired.

For an hour Mohammed pursued his way at full speed over the rough rocky ground, covered here and there with patches of cactus and palmetto, in the direction of the white dome of one of the numerous sanctorea in sight. Upon turning an angle of the saint's house, he drew rein suddenly in front of a large tent, distinguished from several smaller ones by a banner of green silk streaming from a flag-staff planted before the entrance. Groups of men—Moors, Berbers, and negroes, were lying before the tents, or squatted within the porch of the sanctorium. A number of fine horses stood picketted in a long line in rear of the principal tent, and in front of it were several hunting dogs, fastened by ropes of palmetto fibre to a large stake, around the top of which hung several wicker cages containing hawks.

Mohammed threw himself from his saddle, and entered the tent. At his order a slave brought him his writing materials; consisting of narrow slips of coarse paper, a large inkstand of earthen ware, and a pen made of a piece of pointed reed. The young shereef was an expert *talb*, or writer. With nothing to support the paper but his knee and left hand, he was not long in inditing an epistle which, for uniformity and regularity of line and letter, might well compare with the best specimens of typography.

The slave presented his seal, with wax, and a thread of green silk. Mohammed carefully folded the letter, and proceeded to seal it and tie it with the silk, in all the twists and turns demanded by Moorish etiquette.

"And now a handkerchief," demanded the shereef; "and let it be of the costliest."

The slave pulled out from a large leather sack a variety of silken fabrics, the products of the looms of Genoa and Florence; and selecting a handkerchief of a bright scarlet color, presented it to his master, who proceeded with due deliberation to wrap the letter in its folds.

In obedience to his master's commands, the slave now emptied the contents of several other sacks upon the carpet on which Mohammed was seated. The young man, with his own hand, proceeded to select a number of articles from the piles. He chose two or three Turkish shawls, a piece of cloth, richly worked by the Jews of Tarudant with gold thread, colored cottons from Timbucto, several boxes of spices and gums, daggers and swords of Fez workmanship, and an immense bracelet of emeralds and pearls. When these were made up into four separate parcels, he stepped outside the curtain of the tent, and called for the kaid of the stud.

"Bring up the four blacks of Draha," said Mohammed; and in a few minutes four jet black steeds, of matchless form and action, from the province of Morocco most famous for its horses, stood before the prince. In obedience to his command they were saddled and bridled; the packages were brought forth and bound upon their backs, and, led each by a slave at the head-stalls, they were paraded up and down in front of the tent, while the shereef withdrew for a few moments in conversation with the kaid.

"You will take this letter, Kaid Nacer," said the prince, "and bear it to the governor of yonder town. It contains the proposal that I told you I intended to make. Tell the Christian that I await his answer with all the impatience of the most burning desire. Swear to him, by the bones of Mohammed, that I will for ever keep the peace with his countrymen."

"You may trust your servant," replied the kaid; "he will swear to whatever his lord desires."

"And without straining your conscience," returned

the shereef, observing a slight smile of incredulity on the kaid's face, at the mention of a perpetual peace with the Christian. "Hark you, Ben Nacer," he continued, seizing the kaid's arm and speaking in a low tone, "we shall have war enough without troubling ourselves with the Christians."

"The Oataze?" demanded the kaid; "surely his arms can never reach to this side of the Atlas."

"No," replied Mohammed; "the Oataze grows weaker and weaker every day. Soon he will drop like a rotten pomegranite to the ground; and none of his seed will be strong enough to take root. Whose head will be then tall enough to cast its shadow over the whole kingdom of Morocco. The blood of the Prophet flows in Hammed's veins as well as in mine; but, brothers as we are, we cannot both sit on the same throne. Go," continued the prince, "deliver my message; and that you may not present yourself before the Christian empty-handed, take these horses, with their burdens, and say that if he consents to my terms, a hundred horses, still more heavily laden, shall wait at the gates of his castle."

The kaid knew the impatient and fiery temper of his master too well to interpose any further remark. Bowing in respectful silence, he backed out of the tent, and giving the word to his men, sprang into the saddle. The four horses, led by mounted men, were placed in the centre of the small troop; where also rode a standard bearer, carrying the usual emblem of shereefian authority—a green banner. The kaid himself, bearing a small flag of white, put himself at the head of his men, and with a devout "*manshallah!*" gave the order to march.

CHAPTER III.

Fair Inez was seated on a pile of cushions in a latticed gallery surrounding a small open court. A tinkling fountain sent up its slender columns of cool water, which, in falling back into the marble basin, scattered its drops upon a border of flowers. On one side of the young girl lay her embroidery, on the other her guitar. She heeded not the instrument or her work—the sound of the fountain, or the odor of the flowers.

What was the subject of her thoughts? Was she thinking of the young shereef? of his noble form and face—his distinguished air—his persuasive tones? No; she had banished him completely from her mind. She was resolutely thinking of the vanity of human affairs—of the folly of all worldly hopes and aspirations—of the nothingness of life. She was thinking of the air of coarseness and meanness common to all the officers of her father's garrison, and her thoughts wandered, with not more satisfaction, to the awkward, ill-favored gallants of the court of Lisbon. She was thinking that the services and ceremonies of religion afforded the only subjects of interest for maidens in this life, and that she would speak to her father in relation to entering a convent the next time she should be with him alone.

Her revery was interrupted by a heavy step in the gallery. A tall, ghaunt figure, habited in the military garb of the day, except that his head was uncovered, advanced towards her. His face, wrinkled and care-worn, was still handsome; his form erect, and his gait firm; although for more than thirty years had he borne through many well fought fields the weight of knightly arms. He held a letter in his hand, which he presented to Inez.

"Read this, my daughter," he exclaimed; "you are skilled in the language in which it is written, and it is of matters concerning you."

Inez took the letter, and rapidly ran her eye over the fair Arabic characters. The shereef had wasted no words, and his meaning was clear. She looked up at her father, and her face became crimson as she caught his inquiring glance.

"Well, Inez, what say you?" he demanded. "'Tis a well stated proposal, and the young man seems to speak with confidence."

"Dearest father, how can you ask me? It would be impossible to wed an Infidel, even if the exercise of my faith were guaranteed to me; but to renounce my religion—to give up Christ for Mohammed—" Inez paused, and a shudder shook her slight form.

"Methinks, Inez, you take it calmly," exclaimed Mont-Roy, striking the paper violently with his hand. "You look and speak as if you regretted having to reject this offer. By heavens! my blood has not been stirred up for years to such a tumult, as by this insult. But I will send a fitting answer. I will scourge the bearer of this letter from the gates of the town. I will——"

"Not so, father," exclaimed Inez, rising and seizing his hand. "You will do nothing unfitting the character of a Mont-Roy. Recollect that the shereef is a Moor, and that the notions and opinions of his countrymen in relation to my sex are very different from ours. He means you all respect—doubtless, he thinks that he flatters me; besides, were his message an intended insult, the sanctity of a flag must remain inviolate. Reject his proposal, but do it kindly. Tell him that I am to be the bride of Christ—that I am going to spend the remainder of my life in a convent."

"What freak is this?" demanded the old man, completely subdued by the tones of his daughter's voice, rather than by her words. "What has put such thoughts into your head? Tell him that you are going to enter a convent! Never!"

"You will—you must, dearest father—send a denial in as gentle words as possible."

"If you wish it, Inez. And, by all the saints, now that I think of it, if he loves you as he says he does, the refusal of his offer will be punishment enough. I will to the audience hall, and give his ambassador our answer. Nay, do not fear that I will be over harsh."

As the old knight turned away and threaded the courts and corridors leading to the hall where the kaid was waiting, the suggestions of policy came in aid of Inez's entreaties. He thought how ill-judged it would be to offend the young prince unnecessarily, and perhaps provoke a renewal of a troublesome and expensive war.

Accordingly, his secretary was directed to prepare, with the assistance of a Moorish *talb*, a reply to the letter of the shereef; in which the unpalatable substance should be sugared over with as liberal an allowance of Arabic compliment as possible. When it was finished, the governor presented it with his own hand to the kaid.

"Take this to your master," he said, "and tell him from me that I am sorry that I cannot send him the answer he desires. Tell him that I will, notwithstanding, hold myself ever ready to sign an agreement of peace and friendship. Let me hope for your good offices in this matter, Kaid Nacer. Your influence with the shereef is known; you can do much to calm any irritation he may at first feel. As to this present that you have brought, it would be insulting to the shereef to return it; and yet, considering the reply I am compelled to make to his message, it is not fitting for me to receive it. Keep it, then, yourself—it could not fall into more worthy hands."

Kaid Nacer eyed the packages, which had been partially opened, for a moment, with an air of hesitation. The natural cupidity of a Barbary Moor struggled with a sense of self-respect and the dignity of office. The latter, however, finally prevailed, aided as it was by a wholesome apprehension of his master's anger.

With a courtly wave of his hand, he declined the proffered present. "The bounty of the shereef," he said, "is enough to satisfy his servants. I may not receive what the Christian disdains to retain."

Rejoining his men, who were drawn up in front of the castle, Kaid Nacer mounted his horse, and escorted to the gate of the town by the principal officers of the garrison, set out on his return.

The temporary encampment of the shereef was not many miles distant, and by the aid of sharp spurring it was reached just as the last rays of the sun were fitting with golden caps the loftier heads of the Atlas. The impatient prince was at the door of his tent as the kaid rode up, and, dismounting, presented him the letter. With forced calmness he suffered the usual Moorish compliments and good wishes for his health and happiness, and then deliberately taking the letter, slowly retired within his tent. Once within, and concealed from observation, his motions were hasty enough. He quickly tore open the letter, and with a flashing eye and a flushed brow read it three or four times.

For a while he seemed unable to comprehend its import. Suddenly starting, he dashed it upon the ground, stamped upon it with his foot, and then paced with a hurried gait up and down the narrow area of the tent. The black slave raised for a moment the curtained door, and peered into the inner apartment, unperceived by his master; but he ventured no farther. Hastily drawing back, he retreated to the outside of the tent—his face the picture of astonishment and fear.

It was late at night when Kaid Nacer was summoned before the young prince, and closely questioned as to the circumstances of his mission. The manner of the shereef was quiet and composed; but there were indications in his flushed face and fiery eye, as seen by the light of four or five large wax candles, of the workings of the fiercest passions. He listened calmly until the kaid came to the assurances of Mont-Roy of his wish to continue on friendly terms, when suddenly he sprung to his feet, his whole form quivering with rage.

"The dotard! the gray-headed fool! the stupid Christian hound!" exclaimed Mohammed; "does he think I am to be wheedled out of my senses by soft words. Peace! Aye, he shall have peace when that dog's kennel yonder is leveled with the ground. And as to his daughter, I shall not again ask his or her consent—I will take her by force; she shall be the captive of my sword and my bow. I will have her—I cannot live without her. You wonder at this, Kaid Nacer?"

"She is a Christian," timidly replied the kaid.

"True; and you think it impossible that a shereef—a descendant of our most holy Prophet—should hold the commerce of love with an Infidel. You are right; but, once in my power, that obstacle shall be removed. She shall renounce her religion; and, kaid, let her become a convert to the true faith, and she is as much beyond the moon-faced beauties of our country, as the valleys of Atlas are beyond the wastes of Sahara. But come, my mind is made up—have her I will; and to get her, we must tear down yonder battlements of the Christian. Let us lose no time; send in the kaids, and I will give them their orders."

The rest of the night was spent in writing letters to the different shieks of the province, apprising them of the shereef's design of assembling a large army; and in making out requisitions for men, money, and provisions. At early dawn a dozen messengers were ready to ride in as many different directions with the communications of the energetic Mohammed. He himself was early in the saddle; his route lying towards Tarudant, the capital of Soos, where he had appointed the rendezvous of the numerous forces which he had resolved to assemble.

CHAPTER IV.

It was some two months after the events we have described, that one bright morning Inez again opened the door of the turret, and stepped out upon the terrace. But this time a very different scene greeted her eyes. Instead of a few lazy sentinels, the walls were lined with men in arms. Instead of a solitary horseman outside the town, the whole face of the country was dotted with tents. Long lines of horses were picketted in the distance. Bodies of troops—some mounted and some on foot—were marching and wheeling along the slopes of the surrounding hills.

A puff of smoke and a loud report from a heavy culverine on the ramparts, gave the signal for a continuous fire at the works which the Moors, during the night, had thrown up. No answer was returned, the enemy not having yet planted their batteries; but, under cover of the protecting gabions, it was evident that they were pushing forward their trenches with vigor.

Soon the cannonade would commence. Soon a breach would be made; and soon the Infidel would rush to the assault, again and again, perhaps, to fail; but still blood would flow like water, and many a stout-hearted Christian and Moor go down to death in the desperate *melee.*

Fair Inez was too familiar with the details of battles and sieges to feel fear at the sights and sounds around her; but she could hardly repress an emotion of terror as she thought of the possible meeting in the fierce sally, or the deadly breach, of her father and the leader of yon host of Infidels. And mingled with this feeling was a sentiment of self-reproach for the part she bore in the affair. She felt strongly the conviction that she was to blame for accompanying her father to a conference with the shereef, and when there permitting him to address her face to face, and still more for listening to him from the parapet of the bastion. True, she had done nothing that was decidedly wrong in itself, but she felt that her weakness and vanity had brought the Infidels again upon the town.

But what could she do to atone for her errors? Nothing but pray for the destruction of the enemy and the salvation of her friends. Somehow, this duty she could not perform satisfactorily to herself. She prayed, it is true, fervently enough for the preservation of her friends, and even for the discomfiture of her enemies;

but she felt that her prayers were not animated by a holy hate of the Infidel. She took blame to herself that she could not wish them to be wholly exterminated, but rather that the Virgin would incline their hearts to peace, and induce them to strike their tents and make a quiet retreat.

Inez was startled by the voice of her father, who had come to the terrace for a more commanding view of the open country beyond the walls.

"Your lover comes to woo you in gallant array," he exclaimed. "What think you, Inez, will he win his bride?"

"I have no fear of that, father, as long as you command within these walls. Methinks the Moor has tried it too often, and failed, to have much hopes now."

"I know not that," replied Mont-Roy, gravely. "You have heard the proverb, ''Tis the thirteenth fire that cracks the furnace.' The Infidel never came upon us in such force before. Why, how many men, think you, our leaguer numbers? Fifty thousand at least; and what is still more formidable than his numbers, is that he seems to be well supplied with heavy artillery."

"But are not our walls strong?" demanded Inez, "and our men in good heart?"

Mont-Roy looked with an air of hesitation in his daughter's face, and then taking her hand, drew her towards him. "You are a brave heart, Inez, and I may tell you what I dare not whisper to man. Never before have I felt such sad forebodings—never before has this town been attacked in such force—never before has it been so ill supplied for a siege. Had our friends at Lisbon hearkened to my requisitions for men and munitions, we could snap our fingers at yonder Infidel; and, by God's help, we may perhaps do so yet. I do not despair; although I fear the shereef has an object this time that will arouse all his perseverance."

Inez had never before seen her father in such a desponding mood.

"Are there no means," she demanded, "of inducing the shereef to withdraw his troops? Methinks, if I could see him, I could convince him of the wrong he does us by renewing a useless war."

"Ah! Inez," replied Mont-Roy, "I am afraid if you should see him, you would but confirm him in his purpose. His terms would be such as we could never accept. 'Tis but this morning that he again sent to make a demand for your hand. I did not think it necessary to consult you again. We have lived so long in this out of the way part of the world, and have had so much communication with the Infidel, that our feelings are very different from those of our prejudiced and bigoted friends at Lisbon. Still, I would not see you marry him, noble and generous as believe his nature to be, even if he demanded not that you should embrace his faith. No, Inez, fear not that I shall ever propose to buy him off at that price. But come, I must to the ramparts; and you had better retire. The Moors will soon open their batteries, and a chance shot may visit the terrace."

Despite, however, her father's caution, Inez continued to visit the terrace day after day. From this point she had a complete view of the operations of the siege. A spectacle of fearful interest it was to the maiden, and she watched it with feelings that elevated her above all personal fear.

The Moorish batteries were plied with vigor: several breaches began to appear in the walls. The garrison, too weak for a sally against so numerous an enemy, had only to wait the assault. The impatient shereef did not defer it unnecessarily. Morning was dawning upon the high peaks of the Atlas, leaving all below in still deeper darkness, when the Moorish columns were pushed forward to the attack. The Christians were ready to receive them. The noisy musket and the silent cross-bow vied with each other in their deadly work. "Allah Akbah! Allah Akbah! down with the Christian dogs!" was the cry of the advancing enemy, as they rushed up the slope of the ruined masonry, until, foot to foot, sword to sword, and spear to spear, the combatants struggled and toiled in the desperate fight. The morning sun rose in all the calmness of his glory: still the contest continued. The rough stones were slippery with blood; the crown of the breach was piled with dead. New combatants poured in despite the flanking fire from salient and tower; still, not a foot could they gain upon the band of Christians who, with Mont-Roy at their head, confronted them.

Till late in the forenoon the combat raged; when the Moors, finding all their efforts vain, desisted from the attack, leaving two or three thousand dead to attest the vigor and perseverance with which it had been made, and the firmness and resolution with which it had been repelled. The Christians had also suffered severely; but their spirits rose with the retreat of their enemy. They began to have hopes that the Moors would abandon the siege entirely.

These hopes, however, were destined not to be realized. But a few hours were suffered to pass before the besiegers' batteries were again in full play—their fire was kept up with even more than usual vigor. In a few days fresh guns were planted, and additional breaches began to show themselves in the crumbling walls. A constant succession of small assaults was kept up day and night, exhausting the garrison by the necessity of continual watchfulness.

The time arrived when the shereef determined to hazard a general storm. In open day the whole army advanced, headed by the prince in person. All points of the works were attacked at once. Select bodies of troops rushed upon the breaches, while others filled up the ditches with facines, and applied scaling ladders to the walls.

At every point the Christians, reduced in numbers as they were, met them manfully. Wherever the tide of battle pressed most heavily, and at the instant of greatest danger, there was the tall figure of the gallant Mont-Roy, encouraging his men by word and deed.

Inez, unable to resist the terrible fascination of the scene, was upon the terrace. She saw the tremendous rush of the Moors—she saw the firm array of the Christians —she watched the varying perils of the fight with an eye not unpractised in the chances and changes of battle—and she marked with a growing feeling of confidence the wavering of the enemy, and the unfaltering mien of the Christians. Already, at several points, the Moors had been driven back with great loss; when suddenly she felt a shock, as if of an earthquake. The castle quivered and rocked to its foundations, and the next instant there shot up from the centre of the town a broad column of smoke and dust, mingled with fragments of timber and stone, obscuring the sun, and shutting out from Inez's eyes all view of the ramparts. The principal magazine had, by some sad accident, been fired. An awful roar accompanied the explosion, overwhelming for a moment the din of battle. For an instant both parties paused: the Moors in astonishment—the Christians in affright. But it was but for an instant. Urged on by the impetuous shereef, the besiegers rushed upon the paralysed Christians with renewed vigor; and as the smoke of the explosion cleared away, Inez saw with terror that the defences had been forced, and that the Infidels were pouring into the town. They swarmed over the battlements—they rushed through the breaches—the gates were opened, and countless hosts swept through them into the streets.

Mingled with the shouts of the assailants and the clash of arms, there came now up to the ears of Inez the loud wail of fear—the shrieks of women and the cries of children. No quarter was given. Sixteen thousand Moors had perished in the attack, and their deaths were to be revenged.

The noise of the tumult rapidly approached the castle. Inez covered her face with her hands, and shrank trembling with terror into a corner of the parapet. A few Christians, headed by Mont-Roy, made a last stand at the gate of the chief court; but in vain—they were instantly overborne by numbers. Mont-Roy, desperately wounded, was thrown to the ground, and would have been instantly killed, had not the young shereef sprang to his aid, and standing over him, beat back his followers with a sweep of his scimitar.

"Inez!" exclaimed the young man: "where is Inez? Tell me, that I may save her!"

"You will find her on the terrace," replied Mont-Roy.

Mohammed stopped but to order a favorite kaid to guard, at the peril of his head, the life of the governor; and then darting up the stairs, before any of his men could follow him, he threw open the door of the turret, and rushed upon the terrace.

"Come, lady," exclaimed the shereef, "this is no place for you; my men will soon be pouring over from yonder bastion. Come with me to your apartments below, where I will have power to defend you against the brutal fanatics who will soon surround us."

Inez was unable to move or reply. Mohammed, with characteristic promptness, lifted her in his arms, and bore her into the turret. At the foot of the first staircase was a large apartment, where Mohammed deposited his burden, and securing the door, took up a position on the outside. The movements of the shereef, rapid as they had been, were effected not an instant too soon. Already the upper halls and corridors were swarming with crowds of fierce, lawless fanatics from the Desert—owning, even when in their senses, no authority; but now infuriated with the excitement of the conflict, and maddened by the fumes of opium and wild hemp.

Mahommed maintained his position, until gradually he had collected around him a body of his own immediate followers. When in sufficient force, the wild children of the desert were summarily ejected, and order restored in the castle. Not so in the town; all night the work of destruction went on. Every house was broken into and plundered; and by morning not a man, woman, or child, except Mont-Roy and his daughter, was left alive to tell the sad tale.

CHAPTER V.

Fair Inez was seated by the couch of her father, whose wounds, although severe, promised not to be mortal. It was the day after the battle. All was now calm; but it was the calmness of desolation and death.

She arose, and looked out from the narrow window upon the terraces of the lower town. What a scene met her eyes. Wherever she turned, stains of blood marked the white-washed walls, and corpses of women and children covered the flat roofs. She retreated from the window with a shudder.

"'Tis a terrible sight, my daughter," exclaimed Mont-Roy. "Would that neither you or I had lived to witness it."

After a pause he resumed: "For me, Inez, it does not much matter—my race is nearly run. I cannot long remain a prisoner to the Moor. But you, Inez—oh! what may not cruel fate have in store for you! Come closer to me, girl. I would fain speak to you while we have time. There is no knowing how soon we may be separated."

"Fear not, dear father," replied Inez; "we surely can trust the generosity of the shereef."

"The generosity of a Moor!" returned Mont-Roy. "And towards a Christian! 'Tis a poor ground of confidence, my daughter. This shereef has, perhaps, better qualities than most of his kind; but I have little hopes in his generosity or magnanimity. No, Inez, there is but one way in which you can secure his forbearance."

The cheek of Inez grew deadly pale, and her heart almost ceased to beat, as her eyes met the anxious and mournful glance of her father.

"But one way, Inez; and that is——to apostatize—to embrace the religion of Mohammed!"

"Never!" replied Inez, energetically.

"You promise?"

"I will swear it! Put the oath in the most solemn form—I will swear it!"

"They will treat you with cruelty, my daughter; they will threaten you—perhaps torture you."

"They may crucify me, as did the Jews our blessed Lord; but I shall die a Christian."

"I doubt it not, my daughter; but they may crucify me—you will still be firm. What is this world to me—old, wounded, a prisoner? Would not the little remnant of life be dearly purchased by the loss of my daughter for ever? Inez, you must swear by the memory of your mother—by the honor of the Mont-Roys—by your hopes of heaven—that no consideration for my safety shall influence you."

"Father, I swear!" replied Inez, raising with trembling hand a small crucifix hanging from her neck to her colorless lips.

"But, dearest father," she continued, with sudden vivacity, "we may be doing the shereef great injustice. Surely, he has done nothing to warrant your tears."

"Nothing, Inez, but to come upon us with all the force he could muster. Nothing, but to risk his life, and the lives of thousands of his followers. Nothing, but to pile the streets and terraces of this town with the bodies of our friends and fellow-citizens. And all for you, Inez. Now that he has you in his power, will he pause for a maiden's tears? He is determined to add you to his harem—he is resolved to wed you. You, Inez, would not make one of a crowd of slavish women?"

"No, father; but the shereef is noble and enlightened, and perhaps in this he may conform to our Christian customs."

"True, your influence might extend this far—you might become his only wife; for I believe he loves you; but, Inez, he never can, and never will wed a Christian. I know him and his prejudices well. He is at heart a bigoted, Christian-hating fanatic. His very love will compel him to use every means to force you into becoming a Mohammedan. I tell you this, Inez, that you may be prepared for the worst. Pray that I may be in error; but pray also that God will give you strength, through his grace, to meet what may come, as should a daughter of the Mont-Roy."

Inez listened to her father's melancholy forebodings with a sinking heart. Still she clung to the idea that the shereef would never proceed to the extremity of violence, however urgently he might assail her with entreaties. She thought that her father must be deceived in reference to his character and designs. She could not comprehend the selfishness of that love which would compel her to peril her soul. Alas! her ignorance was soon to be enlightened, and the sad forebodings of her father realized.

The day was drawing to a close, when Mohammed sought an interview with her. His bearing, at first respectful and deferential, soon grew tender and impassioned. He told her that he loved her; that his passion had grown by reason of the rejection of his propositions by her father, until power, empire, life itself, were all too worthless not to risk them for her.

Inez listened in silence. She knew not how to reply. She felt such a contrariety of emotions. At one moment she was almost desposed to yield herself to what appeared to be her fate, and confess a feeling of passionate love in return; the next, she thought of her father, her country, and her faith, and shrank back trembling and in fear.

"Listen to me, Inez," exclaimed the young prince. "I know the prejudices of your country in relation to marriage. You hold that it is not lawful for a man to have more than one wife. The law of my Prophet and the customs of my country are different; but I will conform to your notions. You shall be the only partner of my affections. Never will I bestow a look of regard upon one of your sex. Inez, I will be your slave —yours, and yours alone, for ever."

Inez felt a thrill of delight at the words of Mohammed. They seemed to prove him willing to yield everything to her. Her father must be deceived in his character. The shereef would never insist upon a renunciation of her faith. True, he might refuse to embrace Christianity himself; and that, provided she were free, would be an insuperable obstacle to her; but under existing circumstances, and completely in his power, she could not see how that alone could prevent her from becoming his wife, in case he was determined to make her so, and would take her without attempting to convert her to Mohammedanism.

Gathering courage as the shereef continued to pour forth his protestations of passion, she at length ventured to test with a suggestion the questionable ground.

"You forget, señor," she whispered, "that I am a Christian."

The shereef started—hesitated for a moment; and then bending towards her, replied.

"I do not forget it, Inez; though I should like to do so. But it may not be. Were I a common Moor, it would not so much matter; but being a descendant of the Prophet, I cannot wed a Kaffir. I cannot even suffer one to enter my harem as a slave. The whole fabric of my social and political power depends upon an opinion of my superior sanctity and austerity. Were I to wed a Christian, my reputation, and with it my influence, would be lost. My brother Hammed would gladly take advantage of my mistake; the sceptre of the Oataze would pass from my grasp; and it might well happen that the solitude of the desert would afford my only refuge. But besides all this, Inez, I love you too well to permit you to remain a contemner of the true prophet of God. Enchanting daughter of the Infidel, you will renounce your false worship. Ah! Inez, you will let me guide your steps into the paths of paradise."

"Señor, it cannot be," replied Inez, shrinking back, and withdrawing her hand. "You know my sentiments.

I told you them the other morning when you stood at the foot of the bastion."

"Let me hope," interposed Mohammed, that you have since seen cause to change them. Our relative situations are very different now; stone walls no longer divide us."

"I know it well," replied Inez; "but that affects not my purpose. My faith is as much under my own control as when protected by wall and rampart."

A frown gathered itself upon the brow of the shereef.

"Bethink you, Inez," he exclaimed passionately. "You are completely in my power: you are the captive of my sword—you are my slave. I ask you but to pronounce once in public the profession of the true faith, and I, your master, will become your slave."

"It cannot be, señor," replied Inez. "'Tis of no avail to press me further."

Mohammed suddenly threw himself on his knees before her, and seized her hand.

"Inez, I beg you, by all your hopes of life and happiness—by all the love that in your heart I know you feel for me—to grant me this!"

"Señor, by all my hopes of happiness hereafter, I cannot," she replied, in a mournful but steady voice.

Mohammed started to his feet; the frown on his brow grew darker, and his tones sterner, as he exclaimed: "Girl, girl, think what you say. 'Tis no light matter that you resolve upon. Hitherto, I have entreated—force me not to command."

"Command, señor?"

"Aye, command. Are you not my slave?"

"I am in your hands. You can take my life if you please. But when you command me to renounce my faith in Christ, your commands are powerless."

Inez spoke hardly above a whisper; but then there was something in her tone which convinced the young shereef that it would be no easy work to change her determination. The expression of firmness irritated him. Few men like it in women upon any subject.

The shereef was a man, and what was more, he was a Moor; and, therefore, not likely to have any very exalted idea of woman's rights. His eye flashed with the lurid gleam of a tiger—his lips were colorless and tightly compressed. But with an effort he suppressed his rising passion, and once more besought her tenderly not to compel him to exert harshly the power he had over her.

"I will leave you now, Inez," he exclaimed. "Let me hope that you will have changed your determination when I see you again."

"Señor," returned Inez, rising and interrupting him as he was about to close the door, "I cannot permit you to depart with any such hope. I am a Christian:

as a Christian only will I live—as a Christian will I die."

Mohammed paused, glared fiercely upon her for a moment, and then, as if not willing to trust himself with further speech, turned and left the room.

It was the first time that the young shereef had ever encountered any one who, to his face, had dared oppose his will. That a slave should now do so, and that slave a Christian and a woman, roused all the man and the Moor. Fitfully he paced one of the corridors of the castle. Careless of the glances of his wondering kaids and frightened slaves, he clenched his hands, stamped his feet, and gave free vent to the sea of passion surging within his breast.

"By Allah!" he muttered, "I will grind her obstinate will to the dust. Curses on her false faith! She shall renounce it, if I have to give her to the fire and faggot. And yet I am in her toils—I dare not harm her. By the bones of my ancestor! I could find it in my heart to throw her from yon window to the dogs, were it not that my love would make me follow her. By heavens! she must be mine! I cannot live without her."

The next morning another interview followed. It was but a repetition of the one we have just described, except that the conclusion of it was more stormy, and marked by a still sterner and fiercer tone on the part of the shereef. The same arguments and entreaties were urged by him—the same faintly-spoken, but firm-hearted denial made by Inez.

"Señor," said Inez, mournfully, "you say you love, and yet you would make me peril my soul. You would compel me to utter a lie—to assert a belief in a faith which I cannot but hold to be a delusion. You love me! Away with such idle talk. Love—not even the love of man can be so selfish, so cruel. I know that in the creed of your countrymen woman's faith and feelings are of little worth; but not even a Moor could love a Christian maiden, and treat her thus. Señor, your love is a cheat—a sham—a vile, base lie."

Again and again did Mohammed protest the purity and strength of his passion. He entreated—he threatened.

At length his threats took form and shape, and as they did so, they fell upon her heart like a flight of locusts upon a garden—the flowers of hope were utterly consumed. He swore that he would visit the sin of her refusal upon her father. That the life of Mont-Roy should expiate the obstinacy of his daughter.

"The sword is in your power," he exclaimed—"your hand shall direct it upon or turn it from the neck of your father."

"Oh! señor," gasped Inez, "be generous; take my life—kill me with the most horrid tortures; but spare my father."

"And you will renounce your cursed creed?" hissed Mohammed.

"Never!"

"Not even to save your father?"

"A Mont-Roy knows how to die. He would not save his life by the apostacy of his daughter."

"Then, by Allah! and by the soul of my great ancestor!" shouted the prince, "his body shall be, ere the sun has set, the prey of the hound and the vulture. And you, Christian witch!—sorceress! parracide!—I will still find means to compel you to terms. Away all scruple. You shall—mark me, girl—you shall acknowledge my ancestor as the Prophet of God!"

Mohammed rushed from the room, leaving Inez in a condition of mind and body which will be best left to the imagination of the reader to depict.

CHAPTER VI.

The strength of Mont-Roy was rapidly returning; he was able to stand, and even to walk his chamber, within two days after the capture of the town.

With faltering steps Inez sought his presence, after her last interview with the shereef. Her father started with surprise at the change which an hour had wrought in her appearance. Her face was pale before, and her expression one of care; but now, the pallor of her cheek and lip was terrible, while an emotion of mingled grief and terror overspread her whole countenance, and seemed to pervade every fibre of her frame contracting and angularizing the outlines of her round and graceful figure.

With difficulty Mont-Roy drew from his daughter an account of her interview with the prince. Inez feared to alarm her father; and, besides, she felt an almost invincible repugnance to repeating, even to herself, the threats of the shereef. She dreaded to admit the utter want of magnanimity they implied, and she shrank from letting her father see how poor and mean the sentiments and feelings of her lover appeared. But when compelled, in answer to her father's questioning, to repeat all that was said, she still endeavored to screen him in part—suggesting that he could not be in earnest—that his threats in relation to her father had been uttered merely to try her.

Mont-Roy shook his head. "Trust him not: he will do what he says he will. He is not, perhaps, wantonly cruel; but his whole history shows that he has no pity when he has a purpose to serve by cruelty. But you, my daughter, will not be moved by his threats? I shall go to my death calmly, if I know that you are firm."

Again and again did Inez promise her father not to yield to any considerations for his safety.

Her constancy was soon to be put to the test. The tramp of heavy feet and the clanking of iron was heard in the anti-room. Mont-Roy folded the trembling form of his daughter to his heart. He had hardly time for a short and fervent prayer, when the door was rudely flung open, and half a dozen men, bearing fetters and a heavy iron chain, entered. Without a word they proceeded to put the irons upon his hands, and to pass the chain around his body. During this operation Inez stood without motion—almost without sense.

The prisoner was now ordered to accompany his

keepers. Mont-Roy raised his manacled hands over the bowed head of Inez. The action seemed to give her life, and she sprang upon his bosom.

"Oh, father! father! what is this? What is it that they are going to do?" sobbed Inez convulsively.

"Hush! Inez, be firm—remember your promise; and we shall meet——in heaven."

Further conversation was interrupted by one of the Moors, who seizing Inez roughly, tore her from her father's arms, and hurled her with force towards the couch in a distant corner of the room.

Inez sprang to her feet as the door closed upon Mont-Roy, and rushed after him. She reached the anti-room; but not in time. The group had just disappeared, and she heard the heavy iron bolts of the door slide into place. Another door, however, stood partially open—its threshold darkened by the figure of the shereef. His face was pale and haggard; his lips parched, bloodless, and compressed; while his eye, lurid and glassy as the gleam of a deep mountain lake lighted up by a volcano, gave token of the mental conflict raging within. He took a step within the room, but hesitated to advance. With a shriek of agonized supplication Inez rushed towards him, and threw herself at his feet.

"Mercy! mercy, señor!" she cried. "Have mercy on me, and save my father."

Mohammed looked at her for a moment in silence.

"You pray for mercy," he replied in a hoarse voice, "and you have no mercy—no mercy upon me—no mercy upon your own father. You doom him to death, not I. He dies for and through his daughter's obstinacy."

"He would die ten thousand deaths if I were to yield. Oh! señor, think what it is to give up the faith of my fathers; to renounce a Saviour who died that I might live. Could anything induce you to deny your Prophet? Leave me to believe in mine."

The shereef made a gesture of impatience.

"The cases are different," he exclaimed. "Your faith is false; and besides, I seek not now to change your secret convictions. I will leave that to time. All I ask is a public profession of a belief in Mohammed."

"Oh! señor," replied Inez, bending forward and clasping his knees, "I dare not. The lie would blast me. The anger of the true God would follow me. Christ and all the saints would turn from me. My father would curse me; and you, señor, you would despise me. You think not so now; but, señor, I should be unworthy of any man's love were I so weak and so wicked."

There was so much of truth in Inez's words, and so much of pure and simple pathos in her tones, that the shereef felt for a moment his resolution giving way.

But with an effort he banished the rising sentiment, and steeled himself against the supplications of the fair being at his feet. Her very beauty, uncared for as it was by the usual proprieties of dress, while it fired his passions, nerved his heart to the firmness necessary to make her his. He started back, stamped his foot upon the floor, and by the action opened the sluices of anger, flooding in an instant with rage all his better emotions. Instantly he felt himself an ill-used, much-abused man. It was infamous and unpardonable that his will should be thwarted; that a slave—a woman and a Christian—should dare to disobey his commands.

"Inez!" he exclaimed fiercely, "doom your father to death if you will; you know the terms—you, and and you alone, can save him."

"Señor, I dare not," gasped Inez.

"Then, by the holy Prophet of God! miserable daughter of the Christian, he dies."

Mohammed's voice trembled with passion, and he clutched the door with a grasp that left the impression of his fingers upon the solid wood.

"And no common death," he continued, grasping Inez by the arm, raising her from the floor, and drawing her towards him, until face to face, he glared into her shrinking eyes with a look of intense ferocity. "And no common death, murderess!—paracide! Your father dies at the stake."

The shereef relaxed his grasp upon her person. Inez flung her hands wildly to her head, staggered back, and with a groan of heart-rending agony sank to the floor insensible. The shereef paused and looked at her for a moment. No feeling of compassion animated his breast. He would not save her one pang if he could. What were her sufferings to his? Love her? True, he did love her once, but he felt that the thunder gust of rage had curdled his love into hate—he hated her and her whole race. Would that she embodied all of Christianity in her own person, and his dagger should at once end the contest between the Believer and the Infidel.

His first impulse was to leave her as she fell; but there was something unmanly in so doing that prevented him. He raised her in his arms, and carrying her into the inner chamber, laid her carefully upon the couch. For a few moments he hung over her in a different mood—a wild gust of passionate tenderness swept through his soul. He felt his frame glow and tingle with the maddening sensation. He longed to throw himself at her feet—to submit his will to hers—to fold her to his bosom, and protect her against every one—even himself.

Inez opened her eyes, and fixed them upon him with an expression that pierced to the very centre of his soul. Suddenly he clasped her in his arms, and imprinted an impassioned kiss upon her lips.

"You will yield, Inez?" he whispered; "dear Inez! you will yield?"

"I cannot," murmured Inez, as she lay unresisting, pallid, and cold in his arms.

Mohammed started, as if stung by an adder. In an instant the selfish instincts of manhood, and the hard, stern feelings of the bigot, flashed their lurid light above the gentler glow of the affections. He stalked to the door, closed it behind him with violence, and strode off, more than ever determined to break her to his will, or kill her—and with her his dearest hopes—in the effort.

He sought a narrow, gloomy hall of the castle, and hour after hour paced its marble floor with fitful stride. For the first time in his life he felt a sense of impotence. He knew that in ordering her father to death he had exhausted his means of coercion. He could think of nothing further but torture. "I will consult Kaid Boufra," he exclaimed; "he is her countryman, and he has the ingenuity of a very fiend."

Kaid Boufra was summoned. In a few minutes he entered, and shuffling along the corridor with a most servile gait, he stooped, seized the hem of Mohammed's haick, and fervently pressed it to his lips. The kaid was not an ill-favored man naturally, but still there was something exceedingly repulsive in his countenance—the result of a long training of his features in the school of sensuality and intemperance. He was tall; rather fair for one of his country, with an expanded forehead and an intelligent eye, the expression of which, however, was marred by a look of malignant cunning.

"The slave of the shereef awaits the orders of his master," exclaimed the kaid, stealing a look that lighted up with a gleam of satisfaction at the wan and ghastly face of the prince.

"Kaid Boufra," said Mohammed, "you were a Portuguese and a Christian. How long is it since your eyes were enlightened to the errors of the Infidel?"

"It is now six years," replied the kaid, somewhat startled by the question, "since your slave renounced the idolatry of his fathers, and became a follower of the true faith."

"And what was the moving cause of the change?" demanded Mohammed; "or rather what was the cause of your leaving the garrison of this town, and joining my camp? The story has passed from my mind."

A convulsion of rage agitated the features of the kaid; but he smoothed them with an effort, and replied. "'Twas a difficulty with the Mont-Roy. May the curse of the Prophet be upon him for ever! We could not live together in the same town. He was governor, and I but a poor soldier of artillery—he reviled me, and would have punished me; and so I took my leave of him."

"You know the Mont-Roy, then?" demanded the prince.

"No one knows him better," replied the kaid.

"He is of a firm and resolute race?"

"I would say that for him, if I had my dagger in his heart," replied the kaid.

"There is but small chance then of compelling him to change his religion?"

"A small chance, indeed; but if my lord the shereef will deliver him into my hands, that chance shall be improved to the utmost."

Mohammed turned away, and again strode back and forth in a silence which the kaid did not dare to interrupt. At length, as if having made up his mind upon the subject, he suddenly stopped before the kaid, and grasping his arm, spoke in a low tone.

"It is not the Mont-Roy himself that I would force into a recantation of his faith. He may die in his folly, and the black angels of despair may carry his soul to the pit of flames, for all that I care. But it is his daughter whom I would save. You, kaid, have been a Christian—you know their ways—you know the Mont-Roy—you are fertile in expedients. Show me the means by which I can compel this daughter of the

Christian to utter but once the profession of our faith, and name your own reward."

Kaid Boufra's face beamed with delight as he listened to the words of the shereef. An opportunity of paying to his former commander a portion of the deep debt of vengeance he had owed him for years, seemed to open before him. He listened with interest to the shereef's account of his efforts to compel Inez to renounce her creed.

"It was a mistake to allow any communication between father and daughter," observed the kaid. "Her obstinacy is unquestionably owing to him. He has exacted some vow, doubtless, that she feels bound to keep."

"Think you that she would yield to her father's entreaties, if he could be compelled to make them?" asked Mohammed.

The kaid shook his head. Not that he would have disliked to see the Mont-Roy subjected to torture for the purpose of forcing him to solicit his daughter's perversion to Islamism, but he had a deeper scheme of revenge.

'It would be useless," he replied, "to attempt it. "She might not yield even to her father; and as for him, he never could be brought to ask her. I know him well. Against his firmness in such a cause, all our resources of fire, and rack, and wild horses, would be in vain. But there is a plan," continued the kaid, after a pause, and glancing furtively at the countenance of his master, "which may succeed with her—that is, if it meets my lord's approval."

"Out with it!" impatiently exclaimed Mohammed, finding that Boufra hesitated. "I will do anything but kill her."

"I would not kill her," replied the kaid. "I would only threaten her."

"With death? Go to; my threats would be but idle breath," exclaimed the prince.

"With something far worse than death," returned the kaid, with a cunning leer.

"Speak! What devil's scheme is it, that you stand thus waiting for me to drag it from you?"

"Threaten her with my corps of renegadoes."

"Ha! What mean you?" demanded the prince, compressing his lips, and knitting his brows.

"Give her the choice of abandoning her faith," replied the kaid, "or of becoming the slave of my renegades. Tell her that nothing but a profession of Islamism shall save her from the brutal passions of the vilest set of vagabonds that walk the face of the earth."

"Villain!" shouted the shereef, seizing the kaid by the throat, and holding him for a moment to the wall. "But why should your scheme enrage me? By Allah! I will try it."

Mohammed relaxed his grasp, and the kaid, who had made no resistance, gathered the displaced folds of his haick around him as if nothing had happened.

"I will try it," muttered the shereef.

"And if she still proves obstinate?" said the kaid.

"Then, by the glory of the only true God!" returned Mohammed, setting his teeth firmly, and drawing his breath with an effort, "I will leave her to her fate. I will give her up, not to your renegades, as you propose, but to my negro guards. I will abandon her to their lusts; she shall be their slave—their servant—the plaything of their brutal humors. The commonest follower of the camp shall be a queen to her. Her companions shall be of the vilest. She shall wallow like the swine she adores, in filth and sin, till body and soul are alike polluted."

The prince continued in a loud voice, while, with the foam gathering about his mouth, and waving his arms furiously, he lashed himself into a storm of rage. "Methinks I could see her thus with ecstatic pleasure. It would do my heart good. My heart? By Allah! I have no heart. It is gone—destroyed—burned up—wasted to ashes! Cursed Christian sorceress! how I hate her. Oh! Prophet of God, thou knowest how I hate her! Thou knowest how I will revel in her degradation. We will see how her false creed will support her. Sooner or later she will be forced to recant. And then, alas! it will be too late to restore her."

The tone of the shereef fell, and he checked his impetuous stride. "And yet she loves me," he muttered; and I——I——by Allah! I *will* hate her!"

Turning fiercely upon the kaid, who had stood a quiet spectator of his excited movements, Mohammed directed him to go and order his guards to be ready in the morning for a march. The kaid bowing obsequiously, hastened to obey, leaving the shereef to the miserable and irritating companionship of his dark thoughts and fierce passions.

CHAPTER VII.

A SLEEPLESS night for Inez had passed drearily away, but the morning brought no relief. The rising sun lighted none of the darkness of her heart; the morning zephyr bore no healing on its wings for her fevered brow—her oppressed and throbbing brain.

A female slave entered the room, and announced to her that she must prepare herself for a journey without delay. Mechanically, and without a question, Inez rose from her couch, and putting on a few articles of dress which the slave had brought, stood waiting, when Mohammed appeared. He spoke not a word, but taking her hand, led her down the staircase into the front court of the castle, where stood a number of negro slaves with a curtained litter. The shereef placed her in it, and let down the curtains. As he did so, Inez murmured an inquiry for her father; but drawing his head still further within the deep hood of his jellib, he turned away without reply, and motioned to the bearers to lift their burden.

Mohammed mounted his horse, and followed the litter. Without the gates his body guard of negroes were drawn up in waiting. As he appeared their horses were put in motion: loud shouts of "Health and long life to our lord the shereef" rent the air; muskets were fired and twirled on high, and arrows discharged in the air. Contrary to his usual habits, the prince took no notice of these demonstrations of loyalty and honor. Moodily he rode onward, leaving the tumultuous movements to subside into the regular paces of the march. More than once some of his favorite kaids made an effort to attract his attention; but there was something in his air that repelled them. The boldest drew back in affright, as they caught a glimpse from within the shadow of his hood of his sunken eye and hollow cheek. Whispers of magic and sorcery of Obih and the fetish began to circulate among the superstitious guards; and sinister looks were frequently cast towards the litter, which, in as much as it was known to contain a Christian damsel, might well be supposed to be full of all evil and diabolical influences.

The country through which they passed was at first wild and rocky, but gradually it grew more level and more thickly clothed with trees. About noon the cavalcade halted for an hour for refreshments, at the entrance to a grove of argali and olive trees. The curtains of the litter were drawn aside, and the same slave who attended Inez in the morning presented her an earthen vessel of milk and water. The draught revived her, and she raised herself and looked out upon the surrounding scene. There was not much to interest her, save a solitary figure in a green turban, sitting, apparently absorbed in meditation, at the foot of a distant olive. Groups of coarse-featured black soldiers were lying about under the trees. Inez was glad to avert her eyes from their ferocious glances.

The march was resumed; and for the remainder of the day the road lay through a most picturesque forest of olive trees. Late in the afternoon the domes and minarets of Tarudant came in sight, and just at sunset they reached the gates of that city; but instead of entering, the cavalcade turned along the walls, and proceeded on to a villa named Dar el Beyda, the residence of the prince.

This villa consisted of extensive ranges of low buildings, surrounded by gardens, and enclosing within their circuit numerous paved courts and quadrangles. Opposite the front of the principal building were a number of gloomy looking houses—the barracks of the negroes composing the shereef's personal guard.

The litter in which Inez was seated was carried into a small court, surrounded by four narrow, but lofty rooms. The curtains were opened by the slave in attendance, and Inez stepping out, was conducted into one of the rooms. A carpet, two or three cushions, and a copper lamp hanging from the ceiling, composed all the furniture. The slave retired; the door closed behind her, and Inez was left alone in the gloomy apartment. Faint and stupified with grief, and almost paralyzed with terror, she sank to her knees, and bowing her head upon the cushion, implored the aid and comfort of the Virgin Mother and her Son, with a fervor and intensity of feeling born of her great faith and her great fear.

The slave who attended upon her entered with refreshments, and placing them upon a small table, signified that she awaited Inez's commands. But Inez had no commands to give. She simply indicated a wish to retire to her couch; whereupon the slave drew up a curtain at one end of the room, and disclosed a door leading to a small raised recess, on the floor of which was spread, according to Moorish custom, a thick mattrass of wool.

The next day the poor girl passed in solitude; a prey to the most terrible anxiety, doubt—even despair. Still, at the bottom of her heart there was a faint, very faint, sentiment of confidence in the love of the shereef—a single drop of hope. She did not admit its existence to herself; but without it she could not have borne up under her trials for an hour. But even this, faint and feeble as it was, was destined to be roughly driven from her heart.

The sun had passed the meridian some two or three hours, when the tall figure of Mohammed, his face closely enveloped in his haick, darkened the door-way. He paused for a moment as his eyes fell upon Inez, and clutched at the sides of the door as if for support; but he recovered himself in a moment, and with a steady step advanced towards her.

"Inez," he said, in a broken, husky tone, "I wish you to accompany me." And taking her hand, he led her unresistingly into the court, and thence up a narrow stairway into a small turret opening on to the flat roof. The turret stood in one angle of the parapet, and on one side had a window that looked out upon a wide open space in front of a range of barracks. The ground was rough and unpaved; a few thatched hovels, something like large bee-hives, were scattered around; a dozen aged olive trees threw their thin shadows upon piles of dirt and rubbish, and upon groups of half naked negroes. A few women—ugly, filthy hags—each habited in a scanty rag of clothing, but tricked off with bracelets and anklets of silver, were lolling about, quarreling with each other, and bandying vulgar witicisms and disgusting slang with the men. The scene was one of unqualified coarseness, obscenity, and brutality.

In obedience to the gestures of the shereef, Inez placed herself at the window and looked out. It was all a blank to her; she saw nothing in what was before her to interest her—she knew not, cared not what it meant. Her apprehension was, however, speedily quickened by the words of Mohammed.

"I have brought you here," he said, in a tone that sounded like an echo from the infernal regions, "that you may form a faint idea of the fate that, perhaps, awaits you. Choose, Inez, between the Prophet and me, on the one hand, and Christ and yonder brutes, on the other. Choose!"

Inez turned a terrified, but bewildered and inquiring look upon the prince; she could see nothing but his eyes glaring with a wild lurid lustre far within their orbits. Suddenly she seemed to awaken to a sense of the full enormity of his proposition. She started, and pressed her hand to her heart with a look of mortal terror, and then a wild gleam of devotional feeling lighted up her countenance.

"Choose!" exclaimed Mohammed. "Will you be queen of Morocco, or shall I abandon you to the companionship of that ruffian crew?"

"Holy Mother of God!" murmured Inez, "aid me in this my extremity of peril, and enable me to endure all things, unto the end, for thy Son!"

A deep groan burst from the breast of the shereef.

He struck his brow fiercely with his clenched hand, and reeling like a drunken man, turned and descended the stairs. Outside of the house, he recovered his composure with an effort; and calling to a kaid of his black troops, gave him some order in a low but firm voice.

For an hour and more Inez remained in undisturbed communion with heaven—a holy ecstacy elevated her mind above all earthly thoughts. She felt herself lifted as on the wings of light, and carried upward, while hosts of angels and saints descended to greet her, and to hover around her with encouraging whispers and joyful songs. The portals of heaven seemed to open before her, and through their golden arches she looked into a realm of ineffable splendor, and saw—oh! blessed sight!—the glorified image of her crucified Redeemer.

Rudely was she brought back to earth by a rough grasp upon her person. A brawny black stood by her side. Without a word he stooped, and taking her in his arms as if she had been a child, carried her down into the court, where were assembled a dozen of his comrades. Upon placing her on her feet, Inez was unable to stand—her limbs gave way, and she sank to the pavement. The soldiers gathered around her with various expressions of curiosity, admiration, and disgust. They lifted her up, and peered into her face with piercing and malignant glances. The soldier, however, who had brought her into the court, and who was addressed by the title of kaid, seemed to exert a restraining influence. In a few minutes he again raised her in his arms, and followed by his comrades, left the house, and, passing through a narrow lane, entered the open space in front of the barracks. He deposited his almost insensible burden at the foot of one of the olives, around which soon gathered the whole of the encampment. No one of the soldiers ventured to lay hands upon her person; and luckily for her ears, most of the conversation was carried on in the negro dialects of the Soudan. Despite, however, the resistance of the kaid, the women of the encampment pressed upon her, and with coarse words, and coarser gestures, vented their hatred and contempt for a Christian.

Happy it was for Inez that terror exerted a stupifying effect upon her mind. Her spirit cowered into depths almost beyond the reach of sensation. She saw the grinning faces and uncouth figures, and heard the brutal laugh and tumultuous shouts; but she hardly heeded them. With convulvsive grasp she clutched the cross in her bosom. To tear that symbol of her salvation from her seemed to her to be the only object of the noisy crowd—to preserve it, her only hope of safety.

The language and actions of the camp women growing more and more violent, the kaid again raised her in his arms, and bore her into an empty room in a small detached building. Two or three narrow port-holes over the door admitted light enough to show the unplastered walls and unpaved floor. The kaid deposited her upon the ground, and retiring, locked the door.

The silence, the darkness, the coolness of the damp earth—all were a relief to her excited brain and exhausted body. She pressed her head to the ground, and muttered an incoherent prayer for a refuge in the grave. Several times noises by the door aroused her, when she would start and listen, grasping her cross, and with difficulty repressing a scream for aid to preserve it. It seemed to her as if every moment her enemies were about to burst into the room, and wrest it from her.

CHAPTER VIII.

The shadows of the evening were beginning to stream athwart the ground, when a tall figure suddenly entered with hurried step the quarters of the negro guard. He was habited in white of the finest fabric, save that his head was covered with a turban of green silk. The lounging soldiers started at sight of this distinctive mark of the shereef. Who could he be who had had the audacity to assume the holy color of the descendant of the Prophet? It took a second look to discover in the ghastly, fearfully worn face of the wearer, the bold and handsome features of the shereef himself.

Mohammed summoned the kaid of the negroes.

"Where is she?" he demanded with an ill-assumed steadiness of tone.

The kaid pointed to the house.

"And how bore she your visit?"

"As a lamb the visit of a vulture—she cowered to the ground without motion, almost without sense."

Mohammed wrung his hand in agony; but the next instant he grasped the shoulder of the kaid with a force that made the black writhe with pain.

"You suffered," he demanded, "no hand to wantonly pollute her person? Ha! kaid, no arm to touch her but your own?"

"The commands of my lord were obeyed to the letter," replied the kaid. "When I found our women pressing upon her too roughly, I removed her to yonder building, and locked her up in safety."

"Give me the key," said the prince; "and see that your men draw the veil of prudence between my movements and their curiosity."

The kaid produced the key from his girdle.

"If my lord," he said, "will permit his slave an observation——"

"Speak!" exclaimed Mohammed.

"Then I will say," returned the kaid, "that if the Christian is to be made to renounce her errors, it will be necessary to take prompt measures, or she will be beyond all human power."

"Ha! What mean you?" demanded the prince.

"That Azrael is waiting for her; she does not seem to me to be able to resist his call many days longer."

Mohammed staggered backwards; but in an instant he had recovered himself, and an imperious gesture waved off the kaid, who had advanced to his support. With hurried yet hesitating steps he moved towards the building where Inez was confined. He stood before the door without daring to enter. He was afraid to do so—he was fearful lest he should find the predictions of the kaid already verified. Inez, dead! And now, when he had conquered himself—his pride—his prejudices—his ambition for her—when he had resolved to give up everything for her. Dead! And yet he felt that it was a just retribution—a fitting punishment of his crimes; for if dead, he alone had killed her!

He applied the key to the lock, and opened the door. The level sunlight streaming in the room exhibited the form of Inez crouching in one corner. Her hands were clasped tightly over her bosom; her lips moved, as if in prayer. As Mohammed advanced towards her she uttered a cry of terror, and crouched closer down into the corner of the room.

"Fear not, Inez," exclaimed the shereef, flinging himself on his knees beside her.

"Away! away!" shrieked Inez. "Leave me! You shall not have it. No! you may kill me, but you shall not have it!" And she clutched the cross desperately, while turning and shrinking from his extended arm.

"Inez, dear Inez!" passionately returned Mohammed, "listen to me."

"No! no! no!" exclaimed Inez. "I will not listen to you. You shall not have it—I will die for it, as Christ died on it. Go! you shall not have it. I will not listen to you."

"Calm yourself, Inez," continued the prince.

"Oh! I am calm," interrupted Inez. "So calm—feel how slowly my pulses beat. But no—you will take it from me if you come near me. You shall not have it. Kill me, if you will, but you shall not have it."

"Listen to me, Inez," implored Mohammed; "listen one moment. I want nothing from you but pardon and forgiveness. Keep your faith—keep your cross. I give up all to you."

The words and impassioned and imploring tones of the Prince seemed to have a soothing influence upon the young girl. She suffered him to take her hand.

"Keep my cross!" she murmured. "Ah! that will be something pleasant to tell my father. My father? Ha! I recollect—I have no father. You know, señor: tell me, did they not murder him? Yes, yes—'twas you who murdered him!"

"Believe me, Inez," exclaimed Mohammed, "your father is safe—is well. You shall see him again. I deceived you, Inez. Can you pardon me? Can you ever forgive me for what I have made you suffer? Look at me, Inez—not thus. Oh, God! I have driven her mad! Not thus, Inez. Wake up, and look at me as you were wont. Look at this eye, and cheek, and hand. See what a thing of scorn—a shadow of a man—a few short days have made me. Ah! Inez, you know not what I have suffered."

"Poor Mohammed!" whispered the young girl. "He, too, has suffered: I knew it. I suffered, and I knew he must suffer. Every one must suffer. Christ suffered most of all. Poor Mohammed!"

The shereef drew her towards him, and folded her in his arms.

"You shall suffer no more, dearest Inez. Never! never! I swear it! Never more shall you have cause for fear or grief. But you must arouse yourself, Inez: your father will soon arrive. Come, be yourself once more. There are many happy days before you."

"I am happy now," murmured the young girl; "but I am cold—very cold."

The shereef bent over her with intense anxiety. He felt the shivering of her slight form; and hastily wrapping her in his haick, he took her in his arms, and bore her from the damp room into the open air. Without pausing he crossed the square, and turning along a narrow winding passage, entered the court of the vacant house that Inez had at first occupied. Depositing his now insensible burden upon the couch, he hastened to summon attendants. In a few moments slaves entered with lights; several females also came, by whom Inez was speedily inducted into her couch. The kaid of the couriers was summoned, and a message despatched to Agadeer, commanding the immediate presence of Mont-Roy.

All night the shereef sat by her bedside, listening with a throbbing heart to the mutterings of delirium, or paced the open court, a prey to the most terrible anxiety. The sacrifices which love had at last exacted of his pride, and prejudices, and interest, seemed light in comparison with the loss that now threatened him. Should she live, he cared not if he should be compelled to resign all honor and power to his brother, and retire to private life in the recesses of the Atlas, or the solitudes of the Desert.

At noon the next day Mont-Roy arrived, to find his daughter in the crisis of a brain fever. Luckily, the old knight had picked up a good deal of medical experience in the course of his campaigning. He knew that youth and a good constitution are the best of medicines, and that in most curable cases the patient needs no physician. Inez being thus rescued from the nostrums of the female quack solvers attending her, nature had fair play; and on the third day her delirium subsided, and all danger was passed.

Inez awoke to life and happiness. She had remained constant to the end; and great was her reward. Her faith was triumphant, her father was restored to her, and from a cruel master and tyrant, Mohammed had become the most submissive, as well as the most loving, of slaves. Her recovery was rapid; and a few short weeks saw the bloom of health once more on her cheek, and the light of youth and hope in her eye.

CHAPTER IX.

Were our story one of pure invention, we ought, by all the rules of art, to have concluded it with the last chapter, leaving the further fate of our heroine to the imagination of the reader. But, inasmuch as Inez is no creation of the fancy, but a veritable historical personage—one who suffered and endured as we have described—a being once of flesh and life, as well as of youth and loveliness, and now, if there is any merit in piety, and faith, and fortitude, a saint in heaven—the reader may be curious to know something more of her life. For this a few words will suffice.

As soon as Inez had recovered from her illness, she was married to the shereef; the haughty and bigoted Moor submitting to have the ceremony performed by a Catholic priest from the Portuguese garrison of Mazagan. The marriage, of course, created a great excitement throughout the province. It was loudly reprobated by all the *santons* and *talbs*, and learned and pious expounders of the law. That a descendant of the Prophet should condescend to hold the commerce of love with a Christian, was an event that, luckily, they did not know how to deal with. It was an enormity of sacrilege beyond their comprehension to grasp.

Secure in this want of energy and combination among those who most loudly denounced him, and still more secure in the resources of his own fertile brain and iron will. Mohammed soon learned to despise the murmurs of his subjects, and the threats of his brother, who was governor of the distant city of Morocco. There was one danger, however, to which Mohammed grew each day more and more keenly alive—and that danger threatened the life of Inez. He knew that her enemies were busy with their machinations, and that no effort would be left untried to destroy her. Almost daily his vigilance frustrated some scheme—emptied some poisoned bowl, turned aside some dagger. So long as it would be doing God service to take her life, there could not be wanting fanatics ready to brave any punishment in the attempt.

This necessity for constant watchfulness kept Mohammed's love at fever heat, and his passion was fully returned. True, Inez felt that there was a barrier between them in the matter of religion; but she was not without hope that it might one day be removed. Mohammed listened so quietly when she alluded sometimes to the claims of Christianity to belief, that she could not but indulge such a hope. And this hope grew in strength with her hope of becoming a mother, and with the increasing tenderness and care of Mohammed. Alas! her hopes in each and every particular were destined to be blighted.

She was walking one day with Mohammed, in a secluded garden of the villa Da el Beyda. Their path lay through an arbor of vines. The large purple clusters hung around in tempting profusion. Inez stretched out her hand to pluck one, but was interrupted by Mohammed.

"Hold," he said; "here is one far larger and finer." And reaching up, he pulled a bunch that hung overhead, and presented it to her.

Inez had nearly finished eating the bunch, when Mohammed carelessly stretched out his hand and picked a grape from the stem. He put the fruit to his mouth, and instantly started with surprise at the unnatural sweetness of the skin. He dashed the remnant of the bunch from the hand of Inez; but it was too late. She had swallowed a mortal dose of the swift and subtle poison with which all the largest and ripest bunches of the arbor had been covered. The perseverance and ingenuity of her enemies had been finally crowned with success; and before an hour had passed the stricken shereef held to his breast a corpse.

It was as well, perhaps, for her thus to die, before the question of religion had been again brought up by the birth of her child—before her pious heart was rent at the sight of her offspring yielding to the influence of the circumstances surrounding him, and becoming a scoffer and reviler of the religion of Christ.

The shereef, of course, took her loss very much to heart; but his grief did not prevent him from defeating his brother at the battle of Quehera, and banishing him first to Taffalet, and afterwards to the Desert; or deposing the king of Fez, and driving him into retirement, or, a little later in life, from adding every year a new wife to his hareem; or asserting in many other ways his claim to be considered—not, perhaps, a very perfect hero of romance, but very much of a man. He lived to a great age, and was assassinated one day at the door of his tent, while on a journey from Fez to Tarudant. His descendant, Muley Abderrhaman, now occupies the throne of Morocco.

APPENDIX.

Don Juan de Vega, vice-roy of Sicily, having repaired the ruins of Mahede, and put things in the best order, committed the government thereof to his son Don Alvaro, with six companies of Spanish infantry, and good store of artillery, and all necessaries.—Don Alvaro de Vega continued there peaceably enough, taking great care of its fortifications till the end of July, 1551, when the emperor sent in his stead Don Sancho de Leyva. The new governor employed his troops in making frequent incursions among the natives of that neighborhood, and brought in many rich prizes of slaves and cattle. But the Spanish soldiers, not having received their pay for several months past, (though the governor had advanced them subsistence-money out of his own purse, and allowed them a share of his booty,) began to mutiny. They would not be persuaded but that Don Sancho retained their money, which, they insisted, had been always duly remitted. The mutiny soon came to that pass that the officers in general, even the serjeants, were expelled the city; and Don Sancho himself happily saved his life by getting on board a ship there at anchor. In vain he approached the walls with the vessel, calling out, entreating and protesting his innocence. In vain he offered to sell his goods and estate to satisfy that headless monster. Nothing reigned among them but obstinacy and sedition. Don Sancho, weary of his fruitless endeavors, departed for Sicily with his fellow-sufferers. Don Juan de Vega, the vice-roy, fancied he could bring them to reason, but he soon found himself deceived. He then swore to starve them; since they should have no more provisions from thence or any other part. This made them more outrageous. They had formed themselves into a sort of republic, under the direction of a stout soldier, named Antonio de Aponte, to whom they gave the title of electo mayor, or the chief elect, and other subaltern magistrates. Don Sancho repaired to the emperor at Brussels; there to make his complaints: And, soon after, the electo mayor had the insolence, likewise, to send an embassy to that monarch, by one of his own people, whose name was Juan Falcon. What this ambassador demanded was a new governor; assuring Don Carlos "that the soldiery would sooner suffer the cruelest death than have any dealings with either Don Juan or Don Sancho." The emperor read his credentials; but returned no answer for the present; as depending on the vice-roy, who had undertaken to accommodate that affair. At last Don Juan wrote him word that he could not perform his promise; withal counseling the emperor speedily to send a proper mediator, lest the matter grew to a bad consequence. Meanwhile the garrison resolved not to be starved; and their chief magistrate actually governed with exemplary prudence. He armed and fitted out a stout brigantine, on which he put fifty soldiers. This he sent to cruise on the coasts of the Sicily; and it brought in several prizes with corn and other provisions: but he let the owners go without offering any farther injury. He likewise wrote very submissively to the grand-master of Malta, to supply him with necessaries for his money; which request was courteously granted. Nor wanted he whatever could be spared him by the person who entitled himself king of Cairouan, then in alliance with the Spaniards. Besides all this, he made inroads into the country, with four or five hundred musketeers, upon the Moors and Arabs who were in enmity with that prince, of whose persons and cattle he made strange havoc, filling the town with captives and their effects; insomuch that he became so dreaded, that many of the neighboring communities, for their better security, paid him contribution, and even glutted with provisions the weekly market he kept without the city. Thus, there was no great appearance of reducing those revolters by famine. Not that they could properly be termed revolters; but on the contrary, when the prior of Capua, who was then general of the French galleys, heard of the extremity they were in at first, he entered secretly into a negociation with their chief, making him mighty tenders of the French king's favor, on condition he would surrender the city. All the reply he got from Antonio de Aponte was, "That the city belonged to his imperial majesty, and that those who defended it were Spaniards, men who would never take a step in his disservice." This prior was Leoni Strozzi, brother to Pietro Strozzi, who, at that juncture, assisted by the king of France, was carrying on a war in the Siennese against the Florentines and other Italian powers of the Austrian faction. This general had two galleys of his own; and was extremely desirous of gaining admittance into the port of Africa, from thence to infest the coasts of Sicily. The affairs of this city stood thus when Don Juan de Vega wrote to the emperor the second time, as above. The emperor, reflecting on the little good Don Sancho was likely to do in that business, even should he furnish him with money to pay off that mutinous garrison, by reason he was ill-beloved there, gave him the command of the Neapolitan galleys. He then sent for Don Hernando de Acuña, who was at Antwerp, to whom he recommended that affair; sending him immediately away, with strict orders to endeavor chiefly to get into the city of Africa, and there to chastise the insolence of those mutineers with some exemplary punishment; still conforming himself to necessity, and not to proceed rashly. Being apprehensive lest those desperadoes, either for want, or fear of chatisement, might run into some still greater disorder: adding to these orders, that, as soon as these commotions were appeased, he should ruin that place, and retire with all the people and artillery, &c. into Sicily. For as that monarch's hands were then full of many other weighty affairs, he thought it more advisable, by utterly razing it to the ground, to prevent the enemy from ever again molesting him from thence, than, as matters then stood with him, to be at so very considerable an expense, both of men and money, in maintaining it; both which articles he had much more occasion to employ elsewhere. And the better to enable Don Hernando to execute these his orders with the greater authority, he signed him two separate commissions: one capacitating him, of his own proper authority, to pardon all, or part of those mutineers, as he saw convenient; the other a general amnesty, in the emperor's own name: this to be made use of in case the other was not sufficient. Over and above all this, that monarch gave him letters to the vice-roys of Naples and Sicily, and to prince Andrea d'Oria, that they should act in conjunction with him, in all he required, and supply him with whatever he demanded, or wanted. While all these matters were transacting at Brussels, the vice-roy of Sicily, ever attentive to this business, was carrying on a secret negociation with certain soldiers of that garrison, whom he bribed to start a counter-mutiny, and to either kill or secure the ring-leaders of that sedition, as likewise all such as were most averse to a pacification, and returning to their obedience. Of these soldiers with whom he treated, the chiefs were two, namely, Vega and Osorio, to whom the vice-roy made mighty promises of favours and rewards. These, with their partisans, accomplished what there was very little prospect could otherwise have been effected without abundance of difficulty. The truth is, many of them began to be uneasy at their having so long labored under the ignominy of being reputed rebels. And upon this account, much to the scandal of the Christian name, amidst their enemies, that city was just at the point of being stained with the blood of its conquerors and defenders; had they not been restrained by a sort of miracle. Antonio de Aponte, having taken wind of what was in agitation, sent his serjeant-major, a stern, rigid soldier, to apprehend the conspirators; whom he found in a body, ready armed, and determined to make a bold resistance: Their word was, "Let mutiny be banished; and let all traitors die!" While the two parties were forming themselves in battle-array, and just upon falling together by the ears, there issued from the clouds so fiery a blast that the very fowls and birds flying in the air tumbled down dead among them; insomuch that those intended combatants, in the utmost disorder and confusion, were forced to disband; and, guarding their heads and faces with their hands, to run away to seek shelter from those menacing meteors, with whose scorching emanations they were surrounded. That same night Vega and Osorio took such proper methods, that, killing the serjeant-major, who was the main support of the mutiny, and securing all the magistrates, with their most active and resolute abettors, the rest were quiet. Of this success Don Juan de Vega had speedy notice. Whereupon he dispatched the captain of his guards, in a galley, with orders that he should amuse the garrison with hopes of their arrears, under pretence that he was sent to make up their accounts, in order to pay them off. This he artfully did; and as farther commanded by his master, the vice-roy of Sicily, who was resolved that so flagrant a crime should not escape exemplary punishment, immediately sent away Antonio de Aponte, and all his most distinguished substitutes, in order to suffer death by the hands of an executioner. And for the greater security, this officer was enjoined to put into the first port in Sicily he could reach, and there to deliver up those prisoners to the governor, who was to answer for their appearance. The galley got to Alicata; and the governor secured them in a dungeon of the castle, strongly fettered. It fell out that the ottoman Armada arrived there that very evening; and part of the army being landed, the castle was attacked; and, notwithstanding Antonio de Aponte and his fellow-prisoners, from their dungeon, earnestly supplicated that they might have arms given them, to defend the breach, their request was denied; and the castle being soon after entered by the Turks, they were made slaves with the rest. Not long after Antonio de Aponte died of a fever at Constantinople. But Don Juan de Vega determined to have some victims, sent for a like number of the most culpable among those who had not been apprehended, and caused them all to be hanged at Palermo and other cities of Sicily. Thus terminated this affair, which had made so much noise.

The emperor Charles now made an effort to get rid of the expense of keeping up so heavy a garrison by transferring the town to the Knights of Malta. But the order, after due deliberation, refused to accept so troublesome a charge; and Don Carlos having no way to render the city serviceable, resolved, if he could, to prevent its ever more becoming prejudicial to his interests. In the account Marmol gives us of its ruin there are some particulars remarkable enough. The garrison was in arrears thirty one complete pays, (perhaps months,) which amounted to more than 120,000 ducats: and all that the vice-roy of Sicily could spare them was no more than 27,000, and that not all in money either. With this Don Hernando de Acuña, attended by five Sicilian galleys and four large transports, arrived at Mehedia, in order to put in execution what his imperial majesty had directed. He carried with him all the officers who had been expelled the garrison when the mutiny began; judging it requisite to have their assistance, on all occasions; as not being certain, whether the garrison would agree to have the city demolished: if not, it would be proper that their quondam officers should be left to assist in its farthest defense, so that as yet nothing was absolutely resolved on. However, he was better received than he expected. The soldiers flattering themselves, that, besides the general amnesty, which, with open mouth he proclaimed, they should receive their full arrears. But here he found he had occasion for all his art and cunning to conceal from those gapers the scantiness of his purse. The very first step he took, was to learn which of the soldiers had most authority among their fellows. Among these he and his officers privately distributed certain sums. Next he assembled the whole garrison, representing to them the emperor's present necessities for money, and the considerable obligation it would be to their imperial master, if they answered his hopes and expectations in bating him fifteen of their thirty-one pays, and discount from the remainder what subsistence they had already received. Though this set a muttering all whose fists had not been greased; yet those who had been paid for backing this proposal, being men of too good a conscience not to earn their hire, stickled so powerfully for their necessitated sovereign, and represented in such colors the desirable happiness and advantage of being once more honored with the title of his loyal vassals, that the acquiescement became general. However, they expected the residue. This point being gained, they were, soon after, re-assembled. Don Hernando then opened himself as to the article of demolishing that fortress. Laying before them the danger, expense and difficulty attending the keeping it; especially while the naval force of their avowed enemies, the French and the Turks, were actually at sea, and united: so that, even in the ruining it, they must be speedy; which to do effectually, they had no other way but to set all hands to work, day and night, to undermine all the walls, &c. that this dangerous bulwark might vanish at a blast. As to the rest, all he could do, for the present, was to spare them a ducat per man, till their arrival in Sicily, where he promised them, upon his honor, the ultimate Maravedi of their demands, according to the late agreement. To this they likewise consented; and the mines (being no less than twenty four principal ones, to each of which belonged several branches) were ready in a very few days; such was their diligence and assiduity. All being embarked, except an ensign, with two companies of musketeers, the galleys and ships put out to sea at a considerable distance. The orders left with this trusty officer (that all the mines might take fire at the same instant; and to prevent any of them from being choked up by the other neighboring ruins) were these. At the mouth of each mine he posted a soldier, with a piece of match of exactly the same thickness and four spans long. These sentinels were enjoined, that, upon hearing a cannon fired from the admiral-galley, they should light their matches, and, upon hearing a second, instantly go down to the powder, and there put the matches into certain large canes, ready placed for that purpose, and so disposed that just two spans of the match should be covered with powder, and the lighted end, with the other half of it, might be laid clear of it; so that the mines might take fire all at once. Each of these soldiers was farther commanded, that as soon as he had done as directed he should immediately visit his nearest comrade, to examine whether he had done his duty. Of all this the chief direction was intrusted with the said ensign, who was charged to see every thing duly executed. This done, they all hasted away to the boats, which attended, and rowed away to the galleys, which lay a great way out at sea, to avoid the effects of that terrible blast. The first that blew up were those in the west, and they went on firing regularly eastward, and so quite round till the fire reached those made across the isthmus, under those stately walls and bulwarks concerning which the African writers report that Al-Mehedi erected them with such art and strength, and had his mind so fixed upon that work, that he used to say, " If I thought building these fortifications with iron, or brass, would render them more durable, I would certainly do it."—"And in an instant, (says Marmol expressly, who was present at that expedition,) such and so great was the ruin and desolation of the walls, &c. all around, that it seemed as if all the elements had met together to fight in that place; insomuch that in the turn of an eye, this city, once so beautiful in its situation, its walls, its towers, &c. so changed in form that such as had long dwelt there, when they passed that way three years after, mistook the very place. Nay, the strange dissimilitude of its aspect occasioned many great and fatal mistakes among mariners." The great tower near the land gate was left standing; some of the neighboring ruins having prevented that branch of the mine from taking fire. But de Acuña, resolving not to leave it, landed and removed all obstacles; so that it presently fared as the rest had done. Under the ruins of the two towers which guarded the port, were found very large marble pillars, set close together, upon which those towers had rested, and were there fixed to hinder the sea, in process of time, from wasting the foundation: and the floors under them were all paved with fine great marble stones. When the Christians took that city, all the cavaliers of note, who had lost their lives at the siege, were interred in the principal mosque. Their remains were now taken up and conveyed to the church at Montreal, near Palermo, in Sicily. Don Hernando himself wrote them a pompous epitaph, which is there still to be read.

THE END.

Works by the same Author,

RECENTLY PUBLISHED BY G. P. PUTNAM,

155 BROADWAY, NEW-YORK.

KALOOLAH;

OR, JOURNEYINGS TO THE DJEBEL KUMRI.

AN AUTOBIOGRAPHY OF JONA. ROMER.

EDITED BY

W. S. MAYO, M. D.

12mo. cloth, $1 25 ; also, a cheap edition, double columns, paper covers, 50 cents.

"The most singular and captivating narrative since Robinson Crusoe."—*Home Journal.*

"By far the most attractive and entertaining book we have read since the days we were fascinated by the chef d'œuvre of Defoe, or the graceful inventions of the Arabian Nights."—*Democratic Review.*

"We have mentioned a recent publication—Kaloolah—from the press of Mr. G. Putnam—a book in spirit and ability standing decidedly at the head of its class, and only of too absorbing interest, as we can editorially testify from its taking our attention from everything else until, in part of a day and night, we finished it. While its influence on the young may be to awaken, or stimulate too strongly the love of adventure, it at the same time is adapted to call forth noble and generous sentiments, and to show the beauty of moral purity.—*Christian Register.*

"We have never read a work of fiction with more interest, and, we may add, profit, combining, as it does, with the most exciting and romantic adventures, a great deal of information of various kinds, but particularly in relation to geographical matters and the manners and customs of the African continent. The style of the work is picturesque and forcible, the characters strongly marked and well drawn, and the interest kept up with unflagging vigor to the end. The hero is a young American, who, after a variety of strange adventures in his own country, and at sea, is wrecked upon the desert of Sahara—in time assumes the garb and manners of an Arab, runs away from his savage masters, and sets up for a Bedouin himself, and afterwards makes his way through the negro countries south of the desert, to a very curious nation inhabiting that portion of Africa, marked on the maps as unknown regions. The hero of these adventures, Jonathan Romer, is an admirable illustration of the highest American character in enterprise, courage, perseverance, fertility of resource, inventiveness, and capacity of adaptation to all situations. The heroine, Kaloolah, is about as charming and delicate a specimen of feminine nature, as we recollect in any work of imagination or fancy—we will answer for it that all readers will be perfectly delighted with her."—*Journal of Education.*

"We have paid a tribute to the powers of the author of 'Kaloolah' that we can rarely pay to works of its character and magnitude, even supposing a temptation equally strong:—we have read through its more than five hundred pages without omission, and with deep and engrossing interest. We have met with no modern work of fiction that has so entranced us. We apprehend that we betray no secret in saying that Dr. Mayo is not only 'responsible' as 'editor,' but is the actual creator and author of the work. He may henceforth claim a first rank among the world's writers of fiction, and America may be proud to call him her son. The former part of Kaloolah carries the reader captive by the same irresistible charm that is found in the pages of Robinson Crusoe, than which imperishable work, however, it presents a wider and more varied field of adventure; while the latter part expands into scenes of splendor, magnificence and enchantment, unsurpassed by those of the Arabian Nights Entertainments. This we say advisedly, with the full conviction that the intelligent reader of Kaloolah will coincide with the opinion.

"The skill of the pen-artist is quite equal to the exuberance of his imagination and the abundance of his self-created materials. While Mr. Romer's adventures amaze us by the rapidity of their occurrence and their increasing wonderfulness—the reader will pardon the coinage of a word—the equiform gradation of incident and character is so skilfully maintained that no incongruity strikes the reader; and what would be marvellous if told alone, becomes probable and is almost expected from the course of the narrative. We could readily suppose Mr. Mayo to be a well-practiced and experienced author, so much artistic skill and tact are displayed from the starting point in Jonathan's career to his marriage with Kaloolah in the regal palace of the Framazugda. Snatches of sentiment, always of a manly and healthy tone, with occasional descriptive and scenic tints, are interwoven with the web of the narrative, but never to the overburdening of the reader's fancy or the abatement of his awakened interest. Kaloolah is indeed a pattern work of fiction."—*Commercial Advertiser.*

"If we are not much mistaken, Robinson Crusoe has at last found a successful rival for universal popularity. We have never, since the days of our childhood, when we read for the first time, De Foe's master piece, taken up a work so filled with interesting incidents and adventures as this. It is really one of the most bewitching books of the day. Take 'Two Years Before the Mast,' 'Typee,' and 'Robinson Crusoe,' combine their excellences and make up therefrom one narrative, and you can obtain some idea of the character of 'Kaloolah.'"—*Cambridge Chronicle.*

"The crack book of the season; the author has displayed consummate skill in weaving up the incidents of his story, and has contrived to give great vivacity and piquancy to both his narrative and his dialogue."—*Washington Union.*

"Well written, and full of life and animation."—*Baltimore Patriot.*

"Five hundred more lively pages, we have seldom read."—*Albion.*

"We have read every word of these fascinating pages with more interest than we are willing to confess. It is one of the very best books of the kind ever written."—*Evening Mirror.*

"No one can read it without the delightful sense of gratification which it is the province of new genius alone to minister.

"It is decidedly the novel of the season, and of seasons yet to come."—*Concord Journal.*

"Full of stirring incidents and startling transactions, and the author displays no mean power in describing character and scenery."—*London Morning Herald.*

delicately taken up and woven into the composite tissue of the piece with a dexterity that leads you to trust the author in all those critical emergencies of the narrative which are such terrible trials of the ingenuity of the writer and the good nature of the reader.

But the genius of Dr. Mayo is nowhere displayed to greater advantage than in his vivid and truthful representations of the most subtle lights and shades of passion, and the distinctive individuality which he is thus enabled to give to the prominent figures on his canvass. They always preserve their identity, showing a singular artistic consistency, impressing you with their characteristic presence, and this, without any glaring mark of designation, just as you recognize the features or hand-writing of a friend at sight, without reflection or analysis.

The external incidents of the 'Berber' are managed with a good deal of adroitness, presenting a lively picture of the customs and manners of a singular people, so that while intently pursuing the thread of the story, you are beguiled into the possession of a fund of geographical and historical lore which was not set down in the programme."—*Tribune.*

"Since the earlier works of Cooper, there has not issued from the American poet any work of fiction so interesting and so valuable as this same Kaloolah. It combines all those ingredients which are necessary to secure it permanency and a high consideration. Among the very many journals whose critical notices are to be relied upon, we have noticed but one opinion. It is universally commended. It abounds in incident, in narrative, in character: and through all is maintained a propriety and connexion which never misleads or betrays. We are reminded of those old dramatists and novelists whose works are now standards. It is decidedly *the* novel of the season and of seasons yet to come."—*Concord Journal.*

"So clever a book was 'Kaloolah,' by which the author of this work introduced himself to the reading public, that we feared he might prove to be of that class who exhaust themselves by a single effort. We are very glad to find that this is not the case, and that his second composition will but confirm him in the high place he has already taken. His work is good, fresh, lively and instructive. It will be more generally popular than 'Kaloolah.' "—*Albion.*

"BERBER.—The story is more than agreeable—it is thrilling and exciting—and it is related with much skill and effect. The reader who takes up the book will be disinclined to lay down the book, till he has seen the end of it. The characters are skilfully drawn and well sustained."—*Drawing-room Journal.*

"Nobody knows better than Dr. Mayo what constitutes a good story: he is evidently one of the most practical of all novelists. By starting at full speed, and never letting up, the author manages to carry the story through in dashing style, and to the admiration of his readers. The book is a much severer test of his powers than *Kaloolah;* the Berber is a double triumph. Its incidents are what make it so interesting, and give its true character as an original book. In point of plot, the Berber reminds us of the story of *Don Raphael* in *Gil Blas.* The work must have a run. It is more generally entertaining than *Kaloolah,* and cannot fail of as many readers at least as that popular story."—*Lit. World.*

"A romance of the highest class, replete with character, plot, and incident, and occupying ground entirely new."—*Home Journal.*

www.ingramcontent.com/pod-product-compliance
Lightning Source LLC
LaVergne TN
LVHW010220110826
845151LV00004B/1153

* 9 7 8 1 4 2 5 5 2 6 6 4 1 *